AVALON
WEB OF MAGIC

I

CIRCLES IN THE STREAM

RACHEL ROBERTS

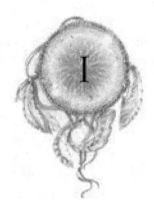

THE BIG CAT crouched in the grass. Dazed, she looked around the meadow and knew instantly she was no longer in the Shadowlands.

Sadness welled inside, threatening to devour any strength she had left. Her world in flames. Her family gone. She had escaped—and for what? To end it all here in a strange world, alone?

The wind picked up, hot and humid across the open field. If she could just reach the trees ... she willed her legs to run, to keep going ... but it was too late.

The creature shot from the sky, sweeping over her in a mass of wings, claws and teeth. Desperate, the cat lunged into the forest of giant oaks and stopped, breathing hard. The clean air cooled her seared lungs, but even that slight movement was agony. She had to move—find a safe place to hide.

A low growl rumbled into a twisted laugh. The creature towered over her. With a roar like thunder, it struck.

THUNDER ROCKED ACROSS the skies, sending the three dogs into fits of howling.

Thirteen-year-old Emily Fletcher tried to calm them. "It's just a storm." But no matter what she did, they slunk low to the ground, growling and whimpering. Usually they were happy to play in the backyard with her, a daily break from their kennels at the Pet Palace. But this afternoon they ignored the ball Emily rolled out to them, pointing their noses instead toward the forested slopes in the distance.

Emily followed their gaze. Her eyes fell over the expanse of trees that met the playing fields and parkland that bordered her house. She had been in Stonehill, Pennsylvania, for eight weeks, and although she'd been an avid hiker back home in Colorado, she'd not yet begun to explore these woods. For one thing, she had no friends—for another, she'd been way too busy. Helping her mom set up Stonehill Animal Hospital and the Pet Palace animal hotel had pretty much taken up all her time. Not that Emily really minded. She loved animals, had a magic touch with them, her mom always said, and being busy kept her from being lonely. Sometimes she barely remembered that her parents were now officially divorced and she was thousands of miles from everything and everyone she knew. Sometimes she remembered all too well.

She ran a hand through her long, curly hair. Animals can sense drops in air pressure before people can, she reminded herself. That must be why the dogs are acting so strange.

Lightning flashed, splitting the sky with jagged forks. Jellybean, the Harrison family's dalmatian, began to leap up and down, barking. Pumpkin, Mrs. Stalling's little white poodle, cowered, and Emily tensed in spite of herself.

"Okay," she said, giving up. "Let's get inside."

The dogs barreled through the side door of the small barn that Emily and her mother had converted into the animal hotel. Emily herded the dogs into their kennels. Biscuit, Mr.

Franklin's golden retriever, walked forward, turned backward to growl, then circled, moving forward a few more steps before turning to growl again. Jellybean threw himself at Emily and yelped loudly.

"What's wrong, guys?" Emily asked, gently pushing Jellybean back into his kennel. "What's got into you?"

Biscuit pointed her nose up to the ceiling and howled. In the back room, a cockatiel screamed.

Something else screamed.

Emily froze, stock still. What was *that*? She waited, her ears straining. Behind her, the dogs were near panic.

It came again, the sound ripping through her like broken glass. Emily cried out. An animal was in trouble!

Instinctively she zoomed into crisis mode. She'd been around animals ever since she turned five, the year her mom, Dr. Carolyn Fletcher, first went into veterinary practice. Emily had assisted in several emergencies: a dog that'd been shot by a hunter, a cat hit by a car. She'd seen the blood and the bones and the suffering in the animals' eyes, and it never got any easier.

Emily ran out of the barn and into the main building that housed the clinic. Her mother would need her help! She raced into the foyer and slipped on the wet floor. She looked down and gasped. Blood. Lightning flashed, suddenly illuminating her reflection in the hallway mirror as if she were a ghost. She stood there, holding her breath.

Shouting from the emergency room made her turn.

She heard her mother yell, "Put it down here!" There were sounds of scuffling; men were shouting, and an animal roared in defiance. Each scream tore through Emily, making her cringe. Still, she pushed her way inside—into pandemonium.

"Hold it still!" Carolyn ordered. Two policemen struggled to hold a wriggling tarp down on the operating table. A razor-clawed paw swept out from under the tarp, raking down a uniformed sleeve and breaking one man's grasp.

"Emily, get the hypodermic!" Carolyn shouted over the animal's yowls.

Emily remained frozen and watched as her mother drew back the tarp. Carolyn's gasp stuck in her throat.

It was a cat. An enormous cat. And it was burned— badly. Only small patches of its leopard-spotted fur remained; everywhere else, the skin was oozing blood. One of the cat's eyes was swollen shut.

"Oh, no, oh, no," Emily thought she heard herself saying over and over.

"Emily! Move it!" The animal twisted in Carolyn's arms and took a mad swipe, ripping the sleeve of her tunic. Instinctively, she jerked back, grabbing her arm.

The cat struggled to stand, but its paws slipped in the pools of its own blood. Emily stared at the awful wounds. Burns everywhere, and, on one flank, a set of deep claw marks. But what mesmerized her was the green glow that seemed to emanate— shimmering, almost bubbling—from the burned flesh.

Didn't anyone else notice? Emily wondered.

"Emily!" her mom shouted. "I need your help, do you hear me?"

Emily looked up. Shaking, she fumbled around the supply cabinet for a hypodermic, trying to get it out of its wrapping. Somehow she managed to measure out the dose of tranquilizer her mother called out to her. The cat twisted hard, letting out an awful cry. The pain lanced into Emily's chest, making her scream. The needle fell to the floor.

The cat was up on its feet, snarling. It turned to face Emily. Glaring through its one good eye, it bared razor teeth and crouched to strike.

Sadness overwhelmed Emily, deep and empty like nothing she'd ever known.

As if in a dream, she slowly moved forward.

"Keep away from it!" one of the cops shouted.

The cat looked straight at her. A hard glint of steel flashed from its gold-green eyes and Emily felt a rush of feelings wash over her: rage, hate, pain, fear and ... something else ... something Emily recognized instantly. Loss.

She stared at the cat. It's all right, you're with friends. We want to help you ... Had she spoken out loud?

The cat's expression calmed, the feral glow fading from its eyes as its muscles relaxed. Emily looked up to see her mother pulling a needle from the cat's side. The animal slid to the table, fighting to keep eye contact with Emily.

Leaning her head in close, Emily heard a whisper, a single word ... *"Home."*

A hand was on her shoulder, pulling her back. It was her mom, her grip firm but gentle.

"Thank you, officers. We've got everything under control now."

"You're sure you'll be okay, Doctor?" one of them asked.

"This is what we do," she replied, pulling on surgical gloves. "Where did you find this animal?"

The older of the two policemen shook his head. "We didn't find it. She did." He jerked his thumb toward the far corner of the room. "Out at the Ravenswood Preserve."

For the first time Emily noticed the dark-haired girl who stood watching, black eyes wide against tanned skin. Where had she come from?

Carolyn turned to the girl. "Any sign of what might have done this to her?"

"No." The girl's long dark hair fell over her face as she edged toward the door.

"You did the right thing, calling for help," Carolyn assured her.

"Yeah … " The girl was out the door in a flash.

"Emily, get scrubbed. Andrea's gone for the day, so you're assisting. You know the burn drill: soak, clean, and cover." The officers had left, and her mom was all business now.

But Emily was frozen again. *Home.* She was sure she'd heard it. But *who* had said it?

"Emily!" Carolyn set down the steel trays. "What's the matter with you? Let's go! Now!"

Emily willed her legs to move. Her hip hit the side of the exam table, making it spin on its wheels. "I … can't … I … " she faltered.

"If you can't help, then get out!"

Carolyn was already dousing sterile bandages with ice-cold alcohol and laying them over the worst of the burns. Emily looked from her mom to the cat, then stumbled out of the room in a daze.

Tears streamed down her cheeks as she walked out onto the hospital's covered back porch. What had happened to her in there? She had *wanted* to help—she really had! How could she have frozen up like that, at a critical moment, with an animal's life on the line? Never before had she acted like that—so clumsy and powerless. She hated it!

She walked into the backyard, trying to calm her breathing. She caught a glimpse of the black-haired girl running across the fields toward the forest. Something ran alongside her. It looked like a big gray dog. Emily shook her head, thinking about those awful burns. What could have hurt an animal like that? And what kind of animal was it, anyway? It looked like a leopard—but leopards didn't live in the Pennsylvania woods … *out at the Ravenswood Preserve* … Is that where it came from? Suddenly Emily shivered as a strange feeling swept over her. It felt like something horrible was approaching … something evil …

"Boo!"

With a shriek, Emily wheeled around—and found herself staring into the laughing face of Kevin Deacon, the fifteen-year-old who worked part-time at the hospital, cleaning out cages and caring for the animals. "Kevin, you idiot! Don't ever do that again!"

Kevin just laughed some more.

"I'm not joking!" Emily turned away so he wouldn't see how upset she really was.

Kevin's mischievous smile faded. "I heard some awful noises a minute ago." He brushed a lock of sandy hair from his forehead. "Some animal hurt pretty bad, huh?"

He could be such a jerk sometimes, but Emily had to admit that he did care about animals. "Yeah."

"Your mom's a great vet."

"I should have—I mean, yeah." Just go away and leave me alone!

"I saw that girl running away as I rode up. What was *she* doing here?"

"She found the animal, a cat." Emily sniffed, calming down a little.

"That girl's really weird."

"What do you mean?" Emily asked.

"She lives in the woods! At the Ravenswood Preserve."

"She *lives* there?" Emily eyes widened.

"Yeah, well, if the town council has anything to say about it, Ravenswood is going to be shut down."

"Why?" Emily asked.

His blue eyes sparkled as he edged closer to her. "It's haunted."

Emily laughed. "Haunted? That is so juvenile."

He shrugged. "Hey, the place used to be amazing. Old man Gardener collected all kinds of animals. We used to go there as kids, feed deer, peacocks, even monkeys. Now no one goes there. They say a monster roams the woods … "

Emily snorted. "C'mon, Kevin, get a grip."

Kevin glanced back at the clinic. "Look, I don't know what happened to the cat in there, but from the screams and the look on your face, it's bad, right? It doesn't take a genius to figure out that it was probably attacked by the same … *thing* … that's already killed a couple of dogs."

In spite of herself, Emily shivered. "Why don't they just talk to that Gardener guy who owns the place?" she asked.

"He disappeared," Kevin whispered. "Just upped and went one day, vanished. Spooky, huh?"

"So who takes care of all the animals?"

"His caretaker, I guess. Some old woman. People say she's a witch."

"Kevin, stop it," Emily shook her head. "There are no such thing as witches." She was getting goose bumps.

"My friend Tyler saw a ghost about three weeks ago, right near the Rocking Stone."

"The what?"

"The Rocking Stone, it's been here forever. It's an Indian monument, like a lighthouse for ghosts."

Emily was trying not to let his ridiculous stories get to her.

"Something's in those woods," Kevin said slowly. "That place should be condemned."

"What would happen to the animals?" Emily asked. But Kevin was already on his way into the clinic to begin his chores.

Emily looked out to the west, where the dark clouds had broken. The sun was setting behind the forest, sending up a fiery glow.

"I don't believe in witches, monsters, *or* ghosts! I'm not afraid." But somehow she was.

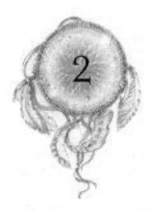

2

EMILY FOUND HER mother in the lab, examining something under a microscope. At the sound of Emily's footsteps, Carolyn looked up, concerned.

Emily paused. "How is—?" She stared at her sneakers. She couldn't complete the question, afraid she'd already seen the answer on her mother's drawn face.

"She's alive," Carolyn told her. "Heavily sedated, but stable."

Emily burst into tears. "I'm so sorry!"

"Shh, okay, it's okay, sweetheart," Carolyn said, wrapping her arms around her daughter.

"I didn't help you … You needed me and I froze!" Fresh tears ran down her face.

"Honey, it was pretty intense," Carolyn reassured her.

Emily pushed away from her mother and squared her shoulders. "I need to see her."

"Okay."

Emily walked to the door of the recovery room and, after a moment's hesitation, opened it. Inside, the room was quiet, the shades drawn, the walls lit softly by a small lamp. The cat lay in a spacious cage. An intravenous needle was taped to its shoulder, connected by a tube to a bag that contained fluids and antibiotics. The cat was almost entirely wrapped in bandages. Its breathing was labored and shallow.

Emily knelt beside the cage. "You're hurt so bad," she said. "I'm sorry I didn't help. Please don't die … please."

As Emily spoke, the cat's breathing slowed and became more even. Its one good eye was halfway open and looking at her.

"I'm right here. I won't leave you," Emily promised.

The cat closed its eye and fell back asleep.

Carolyn walked into the room and knelt next to Emily. "She's sleeping. Breathing's regular. That's good."

Emily gave Carolyn a quick smile. She pointed to a patch of spotted fur on one of its rear paws. "What is she, a leopard?"

"I'm thinking maybe a margay, or some unusual kind of ocelot," Carolyn answered.

Emily stared at it. "What kind of animal could have made these marks?" she asked, flashing on Kevin's "monsters."

"I might have guessed a bear," Carolyn mused, "but only black bears live around here—largely vegetarian and almost never aggressive. Of course, we don't know what other kinds of bears might live on that preserve." She shook her head. "But that still doesn't explain the burns … "

Faintly visible under the bandages, Emily noticed that green glow was still there.

"I've never seen anything like it," Carolyn continued. "The burns seem to spread out from the claw wounds … but the only way that could be is if … " She shook her head again. "If the claws were toxic somehow. Or—"

15

"What?" Emily asked.

Carolyn sighed. "The burns may not be accidental. They could have been inflicted by someone."

Emily gasped in horror. "What kind of a person would do that?"

"It may not be that. There may have been some toxic dumping in that preserve."

Emily's eyes widened. "What if other animals out there are in trouble? We have to help them!"

"Oh, no, you don't," her mom said sternly. "Don't even *think* about going into those woods until we find out what—or who—caused those wounds." She stood and straightened her lab coat. "I was preparing some skin samples to send to the University for analysis."

"I want to stay down here tonight, with her."

Carolyn frowned. Emily pressed on. "Burn victims benefit if they're surrounded by people who care about them."

Her mother smiled. "All right, I suppose it wouldn't hurt."

Emily smiled back.

THAT NIGHT, EMILY dragged her sleeping bag, a careful selection of stuffed animals, and two pillows into the clinic's recovery room and set herself up as close to the cage as she could.

"I brought you Mr. Snuffles," she said softly, holding up the orange lion. "See, he's a cat, too."

The cat lay sleeping, breathing calmly. Emily opened the cage and placed Mr. Snuffles far to the side, careful not to touch the injured animal's bandages. Gently she stroked a patch of uncovered fur on her shoulder.

That's strange, she thought. The cat had two bumps, matching mounds that protruded behind each shoulder blade. They were hard but spongy, like cartilage.

"What are these?" she mused aloud. Could it be a fracture? No, her mom was too good a vet to miss anything like that. And the cat didn't even twitch when Emily touched the bumps. They must be something else, something normal for this cat.

She closed the cage and snuggled down with her other stuffed friends. She was happy to be doing something for the cat at last. She would watch her all night. But the cat seemed at peace now, and Emily found it harder and harder to keep her eyes open. Finally she couldn't fight the exhaustion anymore. As her eyes closed, she imagined she heard a thin, distant voice.

"Thank you."

SUNLIGHT POURED INTO the room as Carolyn drew back the shades. "Good morning, Doc. Rise and shine!"

"Mornin'," Emily mumbled as she tried to untangle herself from her sleeping bag. Finally, she kicked the bag away and stuck her nose up to the cat's cage. To her great relief, the cat's sides were rising and falling with deep, smooth breaths. "She looks better."

"Breathing's stabilized," Carolyn confirmed, carefully laying her stethoscope on the cat's side. She checked the cat's pupils, then deftly inserted a thermometer. A few moments later she was shaking it back down with a smile. "You're absolutely right. No fever, and she definitely seems better." She smiled. "You've got the magic touch, Doc!"

Emily beamed. For just a moment, she let herself think she had helped heal the cat. But of course, she knew that was nonsense. Other than her simple presence, she'd done nothing. Still she resolved to stay with the cat until it was really well again.

OVER THE NEXT few days, Emily remained at the cat's side, chatting quietly or reading to her, stroking the spots of unburned fur. Once the intravenous needle was removed, Emily took over feeding her soft food and liquid vitamins.

On the third afternoon, Emily was lying on her makeshift bed, skimming through her yearbook from last year. Her class would all be starting junior high. Everyone but her. Because she'd known that, she'd made sure to collect as many signatures as possible.

Friends 4ever, Alison, who played on her soccer team, had written.

2 good 2B 4-gotten. Laura had drawn a smiley face next to that, adding Good luck!

Wherever you go, there you are, her best bud, Taylor, had scrawled.

Emily looked around. Here I am. A stranger in a totally new place where school would be starting in about three weeks. She realized she was dreading it. Here, middle school *started* in sixth grade. By seventh, all the kids already knew each other.

If only her mom hadn't found this veterinary practice to buy in Stonehill; if only her dad hadn't moved to Seattle, where his new wife's family lived. The only thing that hadn't changed was having to deal with animals in pain. And she wasn't even good at that.

Emily felt it before she looked up. The cat was watching her. Both eyes were open now, the injured one only halfway, but looking clear and bright within still-swollen tissue. Emily felt a wave of happiness at seeing the cat awake. She dropped her book and scrambled to the open cage. "Hi, there."

The cat licked Emily's nose with a sandpaper tongue. Emily giggled. "Stop that, you silly!"

Trying to stretch, the cat licked tentatively at the edge of a bandage. The recovery process was clearly beginning, but between patches of singed fur, her wounds looked ragged and ugly.

Emily's heart sank at the thought of this magnificent animal horribly scarred for the rest of its life. "You're going to be just fine," she promised. "Your fur will grow back as pretty as ever."

"Well, our patient's up and about, I see." Carolyn walked into the room and over to the cage.

Gentle as a kitten, the cat allowed Carolyn to inspect her wounds and bandages.

"Mom, what do you think those bumps are on her shoulders?" Emily asked.

"I don't notice anything abnormal, Doc," her mother replied. "Her joints may be a bit swollen. Now as for my other patient … "

"What other patient?"

Carolyn lifted Emily's chin and felt her forehead. She swiveled Emily's face this way and that, and stared into her eyes. "Hmmm, pale, needs exercise and sunshine. And I have just the cure." She left the room and returned almost immediately with a soccer ball and dog leash. "Take these and call me in two hours."

Emily opened her mouth to object.

"You've done an amazing job with her, but how much longer do you expect Kevin to handle your chores?"

Emily hesitated, taking one last look at the cat. The cat just yawned and curled up with Mr. Snuffles.

ARROWHEAD PARK LAY at the foot of the wooded mountains to the northwest of town. There were two baseball diamonds, a soccer field, and an extensive playground but near the woods, the land was left open.

Emily, Jellybean, Biscuit, and Pumpkin ran past the picnic grounds and into the meadow that lay before the deep woods. It was an ideal spot to let the dogs romp. Despite the heat, the day was beautiful. The recent storms had lifted the humidity, and hints of a breeze made the flowers shimmer in the sunlight. Emily had to admit that, on a day like this, Pennsylvania was almost as pretty as Colorado.

"Ladies and Jellybeans!" she called, tossing the soccer ball in the air. "It's time for … Doggie Soccer!" The dogs yelped excitedly and began jumping for the ball, running circles around Emily.

"Okay, okay, hold on," she laughed, kneeling down to unhook the dogs from the group leash. Jellybean jumped and entangled her arm. Biscuit had wrapped the leash around her back. Pumpkin was winding in and out of her legs. Emily tried to stand up, but instead fell down, tangled in leashes.

Laughter drifted over Emily as she lay in the grass like a mummy. She looked up to see three girls sitting on a picnic table.

"What a geek!" One, with long red hair, pointed.

Emily felt her face go red as she slowly shoved the dogs aside and unwrapped herself.

The girl in the middle, willowy, with a cap of curly blond hair, stared straight at Emily. "I think she lives over at Clueless Farms. She must have forgotten her pitchfork." That sent the first girl into a fit of laughter.

Emily slowly got up and dusted herself off. She shook auburn curls from her face.

The third girl, the one on the end, turned slowly. Clad in a pink tube top, khaki shorts, and pink sneakers, she wore her long blond hair loose under a studded baseball cap. She squinted. Emily tensed for another snide comment, but all the girl said was, "Hey, that's Pumpkin, Mrs. Stalling's poodle. Mrs. Stalling's gone to France."

"Cool. I'm going there next year," the first girl said

"I'm going to Brazil with my dad," the curly-haired girl replied.

The trio seemed to lose interest in Emily. She walked into the meadow after the dogs. Please don't let them be kids from my school, she thought. If that's what kids here are like ...

She gave the ball an angry kick and it went flying. Biscuit, Jellybean, and Pumpkin shot like rockets chasing down the ball.

The ball came rolling back to her and she gave it another sharp kick. It sailed through the air toward the edge of the woods—and bounced oddly off to the side.

"Gah!"

Emily was startled by the loud grunt. The dogs stopped and looked in the direction of the cry.

Emily ran over to see whom she'd hit. "Oh, my gosh, I'm so sorry. Are you—"

There was no one there. She looked around. Something dashed out between the trees, shaking its head and stumbling as it ran away into the woods. Emily blinked. It looked like ... a ferret?

Bewildered, Emily didn't have time to react. Jellybean and Biscuit were after the creature in a flash, letting loose a chorus of barks. Pumpkin sat and wagged her tail.

"Hey! Wait!" Emily yelled. "Come back here!" But the

dark forest seemed to swallow her cries.

She felt a weird chill come over her. She hesitated. She didn't believe Kevin's nonsense about haunted woods and scary monsters. Just the same, she felt a tingle along the back of her neck. But the dogs were her responsibility. She had no choice. She had to find them!

Emily attached the leash to Pumpkin's collar. "It'll take more than a few haunted trees to stop us," she said, faking a courage she didn't feel. The little poodle lunged forward eagerly, pulling Emily into the dark shade of the trees. "To the haunted woods!"

There was no turning back now.

THE LAND SLOPED gradually uphill and, after awhile, Emily had to stop and catch her breath. She cautiously looked around. Nothing seemed remotely haunted about this forest. It was just trees, undergrowth, and lots of shade. Just like hiking in the Rockies back home—her *old* home, she corrected herself.

"We've got to find a trail." Her voice fell flat in the stillness of the woods.

As if in answer, Pumpkin pushed on straight through the underbrush.

Emily bent forward, with one arm held up as a shield. "Or we could go your way." Branches whipped at her legs and scratched her face, and then they were through and onto a narrow but well-worn path.

"Good job!" Emily exclaimed. "Pumpkin, are you part bloodhound?"

Pumpkin yapped and tugged at the leash. Emily allowed the poodle to pull her briskly up the path. Thick trees and lush plant growth surrounded her. It was hard to take Kevin's stories seriously as she breathed in the sweet smells of the forest—but it was also hard to forget the terrible burns on the cat and her mother's fears that someone might be in these woods, hurting animals. The cool air turned damp on her skin and she shivered.

She could no longer hear the other dogs barking. She hoped that didn't mean they'd caught the ferret. Or worse, that something had caught *them.*

"Come on," she told Pumpkin. "Find Biscuit and Jellybean."

Pumpkin followed the trail. On either side, the woods seemed to be getting darker and more ominous. Emily was straining to hear any signs of the runaway dogs. The rustle of leaves made her look around nervously. Light and shadows played in and out of the trees. Twisted overhanging branches seemed to reach out for her. The trail led around the side of a hill, curved to the left and then spilled out onto a dirt road. Emily slid down a sudden incline, piling right into Pumpkin. She looked up. A large stone arch with twin iron gates was in front of her. On either side of the arch stretched a tall stone wall. The gates were closed. Emily stared in dismay. The dogs could be anywhere. There was a sign on the wall next to the arch. She walked over to read it.

RAVENSWOOD WILDLIFE PRESERVE
Open 11 AM to Duh

Emily giggled as she realized that vines had grown over the last letters on the sign and arranged themselves to look like an "h." She pulled the vines aside and read again:

Open 11 AM to Dusk.
Please don't feed the animals, and stay on the paths.

Garbage in, garbage out policy. $200 fine for littering.

"Wow, this is it! The wildlife preserve!"

Emily glanced at her watch: 11:30 A.M., but the gate was closed. Then she remembered what Kevin said about the old man disappearing. Maybe there *was* no one to keep the place open now. Except a caretaker who happened to be a witch!

"Rrrroof!"

The sound came from the other side of the wall. She grabbed the iron bars and jumped up on the gate, trying to peer farther into the estate. No sign of any dogs.

"Rrrouff!"

They must have gotten through somehow.

"Get back here!" she called sternly. But there was no response. She was starting to feel queasy. "Maybe we could find a way in somewhere else—"

Creeaaaakkk ...

The sudden sound of metal on metal startled her as the heavy gate began to swing open. She hung on. "You have visitors," she said nervously.

She jumped off the gate onto the road on the other side. "Jellybean! Biscuit!" She really hoped they'd come bounding out of the woods so she wouldn't have to go in after them. But neither dog appeared.

Emily drew in a breath. What if whatever had mauled the cat was still here? Hadn't Kevin said a few neighborhood dogs that had wandered in had been—*no*! Emily shook her head. She was so not going there. She'd find the dogs. And they'd be fine.

There seemed to be two ways to go: the main road, or a smaller path that led off to the left. "Which way?"

Pumpkin pulled her along the smaller path. Emily's heart began to beat faster.

The woods closed around the path, deeper and thicker. The air smelled of damp earth. She called again, "Biscuit! Jellybean!"

She thought she heard a few woofs in the distance, but she couldn't tell which direction they were coming from. She had a fleeting sense that something was following her. A soft rustling startled her. She turned to her right and thought she saw the strangest thing: a white mist snaking through the trees. A ghost? There was a loud squawk, and a flash of green and red and purple flew between the tree branches. Tropical birds, she thought, certainly not native to these woods. When she looked back, the mist was gone. Must have been a trick of the light, she told herself.

"Arff!"

Pumpkin pointed to the right. Emily saw a shadow move between the trees.

"Who's there?" she called out, her pulse pounding in her ears. This was getting really creepy. A rustling in the undergrowth startled her and she whirled around to see the back of a very large animal as it disappeared from view. What was *that*? A moose? No, stupid, there're no moose in Pennsylvania. Oh yeah, right, this is a wildlife preserve. Who knows what kind of animals are here? In fact, who even knew *she* was here? She was all alone in the *haunted* woods … Okay, she told herself, calm down, don't panic.

As she led Pumpkin down the other path, visions of "haunted woods" and the old witch who lived there sprang up as in those Grimm's fairy tales that had scared her when she was young. The hairs on the back of her neck stood up. Turning around, Emily saw the white mist again. It was moving, snaking through the trees straight toward her. "Oh, no … this is not good … "

She ran up a little rise, then stopped to look over her shoulder. The wavering white mist was still there, getting thicker and closer. She scooped up Pumpkin and started to walk faster—then she broke into a run.

Low-hanging branches caught at her clothes, scratching at her arms and legs. This was all too weird and crazy, Emily kept thinking. She was just letting herself be spooked by what Kevin had said. But the cat—the cat was real. She was starting to panic. She had trouble catching her breath, but she couldn't stop running.

"Help! Help!" she cried out, but her screams were swallowed by the dark and hungry forest. She was in deep woods now. She stumbled over tree roots, pushed through the undergrowth—turning her head, she saw the white mist right behind her. For a split second, Emily froze. She willed her legs to move, to run. But she'd only taken a few steps when she tripped over something and did a face plant into the ground.

There was a yelp and then she realized what she had fallen over—Jellybean! Her heart leaped. He was totally fine. Nothing had mauled him. A second later Biscuit came trotting up and licked her face. Relief flooded through her.

"Bad dogs!" She scolded them half-heartedly—and stopped.

There, under a natural archway formed by trees, was a wolf. Its fur was silver, fading to white. Its eyes, rimmed in charcoal, were warm gold. It sat perfectly still, staring back at Emily. Then it stood and turned to walk through the archway. Jellybean and Biscuit followed.

"Hey, wait!" Emily called. She probably should be scared, but she wasn't.

With Pumpkin close at her side, Emily walked through the archway. The wolf was nowhere in sight. But something else definitely was. Beyond the archway stood the largest boulder she had ever seen. She craned her neck to look at the stone tower, following it up to a jagged peak that pointed into the sky. It was so tall, she wondered why she hadn't noticed it looming up above the trees.

"Wow," Emily breathed. "It's the Rocking Stone." So Kevin was right about one thing, anyway. The rock was *amazing*. Lines of quartz glistened all around the sides, catching the sunlight. When she looked more closely, she could see markings that looked like graffiti.

"Look what you guys found!" she exclaimed to the dogs.

She stepped around the rock—and saw what it was hiding. A magnificent forest glade surrounded by a perfect circle of tall firs. In the glade's center, a pond shimmered like a sky-blue mirror, except where willows brushed the water with the tips of their flowing branches. At the far side, a rippling stream flowed into the forest and a small bridge arched across the water. Songbirds trilled in the treetops. Golden sunlight poured through the trees. This was the most beautiful place she'd ever seen!

"Ruff-chooo!" Pumpkin sneezed. She had stopped to sniff something.

Looking down, Emily saw a clump of incredible flowers: small, fuzzy puffs of every imaginable color!

She bent down and picked one of the flowers. It looked like a sparkly dandelion. She blew on it and tiny glittering tufts danced away on the breeze.

"I might have just discovered a whole new species. Genus: Emily," she laughed.

"Yipp!"

"Okay, okay. Genus: Pumpkin."

Emily felt like an explorer discovering a new world. Suddenly three animals stepped out of the trees. Emily stopped and held her breath. They looked like deer, but not like any deer Emily had ever seen. They had green striped fur and purple eyes. They bent their heads gracefully to drink from the pond, then looked up and scampered away. Emily shook her head. Deer aren't green! Must have been the sunlight reflected off the water. A bright red bird—could that really be a scarlet macaw?—flapped from a treetop to a lower branch, where it joined another bird, this one purple and orange. These creatures seemed so peaceful, so comfortable in their surroundings, not even bothered by the dogs. Surely there could be no dangerous predator around.

Slowly, so as not to startle the animals, Emily walked to a flat rock at the edge of the pond and sat down. She pulled off her sneakers and socks, stuck her feet in the water, and splashed her toes lazily. Her reflection swirled in the water. It felt so refreshing, clean, and cold, like a mountain pool. She dashed some on her face, then flicked water at Biscuit. With a bark, Jellybean took a flying leap and landed in the pond, sending water cascading all around. Emily threw water at Pumpkin, who ran around barking happily.

And the water turned pink.

Emily stared. Bright colors—orange, purple, red—began to bubble up, sending soft circles out across the pool. The colors deepened, becoming darker and richer. Emily jerked her feet out of the water. Then she saw something under the surface, glowing.

Leaning over, she stuck her hand in the water, reaching … The tips of her fingers bumped against something small, cold, and hard in the wet clay. Her hand closed around the object and her stomach lurched. She felt as if she had just taken the first drop in Gigantor, the huge wooden roller coaster that used to terrify her.

There was a loud rustling in the forest. Terrified, Emily scrambled to her feet, looking around. The dogs pressed tightly against her legs, whimpering. What was happening?

Wind whipped across the glade, sending up small eddies of dried leaves and dirt. Three, four, then six tiny whirlpools spiraled and twirled across the grass. One spun right by Emily's legs and, out of the corner of her eye, she thought she saw a figure. A figure made of twigs, dirt, and leaves? A sound buzzed from the swirling debris.

"Beeeeeeeeeeeeeee … "

"What?"

"Bbeeeeeeewrrrrrrrrrrr … " Another mini-tornado twirled by, sending pebbles and bits of dirt flying. Squinting against the dust, Emily stood stock-still as a third little whirlwind spun crookedly by her leg.

"Beeeewaaarre … " it hummed.

The shrieking wind grew louder, scattering the figures across the glade. Tree limbs snapped and came crashing to the ground. Emily sank to her knees, wrapping her arms tightly around the dogs. Frantically she looked about for a place—any place—to hide. Then she saw it—and her heart stopped. A dark purple shape loomed up through the trees, making its way straight for her and the dogs. She whirled around—and saw the ghostly mist flow from between two trees and seep into the glade. It was about to envelop her, and there was nothing she could do. She was trapped. Her heart was in her throat; she couldn't breathe. The mist fell silently over Emily and the dogs, covering them in a soft blanket. The dogs shivered. She hugged them close, soundlessly willing them to keep quiet. Through the misty veil she saw a shadow move past. It looked like a giant dark purple bear. Emily didn't know why, but for a moment she wasn't frightened. She allowed herself to breathe.

Boom!

The ground rocked. Something had fallen out of the sky! Something big. The earth around her trembled from the impact. The wind kicked up again, as if blasted by the beating of great wings. The air itself seemed to twist, a wobbling spiral that made Emily sick to her stomach. She sensed animal cries of terror, creatures frantically fleeing through the brush.

Emily didn't move. The thing that fell from the sky was some kind of animal. No, *creature*. She could feel it probing, searching for prey. Whatever it was, it was no bear; she was sure of that. It was bigger, more dangerous. It moved slowly around the glade, snorting and growling.

Emily huddled in the thick mist with the dogs tight against her. She was so frightened she could hardly think. The dogs were wriggling and starting to whine. Trembling, she pulled out the group leash and, one by one, hooked up each dog. "Shhhhh," she whispered. But she fumbled the last hook, and it closed with an audible *snap!*

The creature whirled and came straight toward them. Emily's heart pounded like a sledgehammer. Even through the misty veil, she could see the faint outlines of long, sharp claws, monstrous wings, and red-hot glowing eyes.

She could smell it, too, something rotten. She was going to gag. She closed her eyes as a blood-curdling roar made the dogs whimper. There was a beating of great wings, a rush of hot air—and the creature took off, disappearing into the sky.

Then all was quiet. Emily opened her eyes—and stared straight into the eyes of the silver wolf. They blazed with gold fire. She wanted to scream, but nothing came out.

"Do not be afraid." She heard no sound, and yet she understood the voice perfectly. *"You are safe for now."*

Emily blinked and shook her head. The dogs were staring at the wolf, amazingly calm, as if they, too, had heard the reassuring words.

A tightness in her arm made her realize she'd been clenching her fist all this time. She opened her hand and saw that the object she'd picked up from the water was in her palm. It was a small, rough, dark stone.

She looked back to the wolf, but it had disappeared again. What had just happened? What was that flying ... *thing?*

Without another thought, she pulled on her shoes, grabbed the leash, and ran as fast as she could, back past the Rocking Stone, back the way she'd come. The dogs galloped ahead and she let them pull her along. Soon she was back at the dirt trail and followed it to the main road out of the preserve.

The farther she got from the woods, the more the whole thing felt like a dream. Ghosts weren't real. Wolves didn't talk. There were no rainbow flowers. And huge flying monsters? Was *that* what had attacked the cat? She shuddered.

Biting her lip, she sped up again, tugging on the leash. She was *not* going to think about any of this weirdness anymore. She was going to go straight home, where she belonged.

4

"UNABLE TO LOCATE server. Please check the server name and try again."

Shoot! Emily sat at her desk, staring at the computer screen.

As soon as she'd gotten home and cleaned herself up, she'd gone online, trying various search engines to track down information on the Ravenswood Wildlife Preserve. But either the links had the address wrong or the website no longer existed.

She couldn't ask her mom for help—she didn't want to explain about almost losing the dogs and going into the woods.

She thought of e-mailing her dad. He was a scientist. He'd know what to do. But what would she say? "Dear Dad, having a terrific time here. Today I met a monster and a ghost and I discovered some new flower with rainbow seeds that light up like tiny fireworks … " Ha! Her dad would think she had moved to Transylvania, not Pennsylvania.

Okay, think … "If one thing doesn't work," he'd say, "then try another way." She typed in "Rocking Stone." A page of sites came back. "Indian Totems." She hit the hot link button.

The site was part of a Web ring dedicated to Native American legends and stories. She skimmed down the listing. There it was: "The Rocking Stone." A sacred monument called "Aluns," a Lenni Lenape name which means "arrow." Such stones were believed to be landmarks used to locate doorways to the spirit world ...

She sat back. Those woods were haunted, all right. Kevin had not been wrong about that. So*mething* was going on out there! But what had happened to her today was simply not possible. She had to have imagined it. Except she hadn't imagined the cat. Something evil had attacked it. And whatever it was, it was still out there.

"HEALER ... "

"What—who are you?" She walked through silver-white fog. Faint outlines of trees shifted in the corners of her vision. She had an impression that animals were hiding in the swirling mist, watching her.

A chorus of voices called to her. "Healer ... help us ... "

"I'm not a healer!" she cried in frustration. "I don't know how to help you!"

Waves of color swirled violently. The voices vanished as razor claws ripped away the misty curtain. The monster snarled, revealing a mouth full of dripping fangs. Red-hot demon eyes fixed on her. It knew she was helpless! With a roar it attacked—

Emily bolted up in bed as her eyes flew open, her mouth agape in a silent, choked-off scream. Her Pooh night-light glowed softly near the door. She fought to calm her breathing. It was only a dream, it wasn't real ... Something else was glowing in the room, and it wasn't coming from the night-light. Emily quietly slipped from her bed and padded over to the pile of clothes she had thrown off earlier. She stared. The glow came from the pocket of her shorts. She reached inside. A pulsing blue-green washed over her face as she pulled out the stone she had found at the glade. It felt warm and reassuring in her hand—smooth and slick to the touch. Smooth? The stone she'd plucked from the pond had been rough!

Somehow most of the crusty layers had vanished. The stone was shiny and faceted in places. The blue-green surface was shot with clear, sparkly veins of purple. She turned it over and over. How could she not have noticed how pretty it was when she found it?

It felt … magical.

"Ridiculous!" she snorted.

She sat holding the stone, looking at it for answers. But no matter how hard she tried, she couldn't think of anything that didn't sound completely insane. Maybe it was radioactive, or part of a meteor, but it felt so … right. More strange things had happened to Emily today than in the whole rest of her life. She hated things she couldn't explain! *Everything* had a scientific explanation, didn't it? Okay, so what *had* really happened?

She knew what she had to do. Regardless of what might be in those woods, she was going back, back to that glade to find some answers for herself.

THE SUN HAD risen, but the dew still sparkled on the grass. It was going to be another beautiful day. Emily walked across the park and playing fields, her long shadow stretching ahead of her as she followed it westward. It fell to her right when she turned up the main road to the Ravenswood Wildlife Preserve. As she approached the iron gate, she hesitated.

What was she doing? Last time she'd *had* to go in there —she'd had no choice. This time she was going back on purpose—and she knew it might not be safe.

Emily was terrified. Had she actually seen a monster in those woods? She thought of the glowing stone. *Could* it be radioactive? Was someone doing experiments on the animals there?

She squared her shoulders. She was determined to find that glade. She'd stick to clear trails. Any sign of trouble, she'd turn back immediately.

She swung the heavy iron gate open and passed through.

This time she followed the main road. There was no sign of the magical puff flowers. And no sign of the ghosty mist, either. The path turned into a pebble driveway that sloped downward through an expansive lawn. And at the far end stood the imposing structure of an incredible mansion, nestled in the woods. As Emily approached, it rose up like an ancient castle complete with ivy covered, stone turrets. The main house was huge, and there were smaller buildings that could have been guesthouses or stables. Two large front windows seemed to watch her like dark eyes. She had the oddest feeling that the house itself was alive.

Yeah, right! Houses were *not* alive. A light flared from a second-story window. That was strange. Could Mr. Gardener have returned? Or maybe it was a witch with a big cauldron! Maybe she was a good witch, like Glinda. Or maybe she ate little children like in Hansel and Gretel. Stop it! Emily scolded herself. You're being silly. Those're fairy tales, kid stuff.

Then she heard the scream.

5

"OWEEEIIIOO!"

What was *that*? Someone was in pain!

"Ooooweeeiooooo!"

Frantically Emily looked around. The high-pitched moan was coming from somewhere in the woods!

"Heeellp!"

Emily turned and ran in the direction of the voice. She zigzagged through the trees, making her way around thorny thickets and muddy hollows. The cries were nearer now and more distinct.

"Ow! Ow! Heeelllppp—gah!"

Emily crashed into a small clearing—and stopped, panting hard. Kneeling by a tree was a girl. She had her back toward Emily as if doubled over in pain. Long, shiny black hair fell over her dark T-shirt. She wore black jeans and hiking boots.

"Are you okay?" Emily gasped, out of breath.

The girl turned her head, fixing startled dark eyes on Emily. It was that strange girl who'd brought the wounded cat to the clinic. "What do you think you're doing here?" she

40

demanded.

Emily moved back a step. "I ... I ... you called for help," she said, confused by the girl's hostility.

"I did not!" The girl was crouched over something. "This is private property. Get out of here!"

Emily wasn't about to be intimidated again. "And what gives *you* the right to be here?" she shot back.

"I *live* here," she said.

Emily tried to peer over the girl's shoulder. "What's that you've got there?"

"Nothing," she insisted, maneuvering her body between Emily and whatever she was hiding.

Emily edged closer.

"Go home!" the girl demanded, dark eyes flashing. "You don't belong here."

"Neither do I!" exclaimed a high-pitched voice. "And whatever I am, I'm certainly not nothing. Ow, my leg! Ow-ow-owwwie!!!"

Emily faked to the left, then twisted around to her right. Before the other girl knew it, Emily was past her.

She blinked, totally surprised. In front of her, a golden ferret writhed in pain, his foot caught in a steel trap that was way too big for his elongated, furry body. "He needs help!" Emily exclaimed.

"That's what I was trying to do, genius," the girl replied.

Emily bent over to examine the ferret closer. His fur was mostly pale gold with wisps of brown; his feet, tail tip, and mask were darker brown.

"Watch out, he'll bite you," the girl warned.

Cautiously, Emily reached down to find a good grip on the trap.

41

"Owwie, owwwie … ow—Aghhh!!!!"

"Hold still a minute," she told the ferret. "I haven't done anything yet."

"Oh. Well, get on with it."

Emily's jaw dropped. She stared at the ferret. "It's … it can't be—but I think he's *talking!*"

"Score one for you," the girl replied.

Emily tried to pull apart the steel jaws, but she wasn't strong enough. The other girl reached out to help. Together, they pulled the trap open just enough for the creature to wiggle his foot free.

"Oh, that feels so gooooood! I could kiss you, but I'm not sure I even have lips."

Emily's head whirled. This was impossible!

The ferret sat and examined his foot. "What in the world am I?" he asked, alarmed. "I look like some sort of *rodent*!" He stood and hobbled. "Aaahhh! How could they do this to me?" Then he looked up at Emily and his small eyes, set inside the brown mask, blinked. "Hey, aren't you the one who hit me on the head with that big rock?"

"It was a soccer ball," she corrected distractedly. Wait a minute! She was correcting a *ferret*!

"Is that some kind of formal greeting here? Beaning me on the head?"

"It was an accident."

"What kind of world is this? Everything hurts!" the ferret whined.

"What's he talking about?" the other girl asked. "You hit him?"

"No, I mean, yes, I—" Emily stopped suddenly. "But—but—that means … " She sat down hard on the ground. "If we can *both* hear him, then it must really—I mean, can it be talking?" She shook her head. "No way! Not possible!"

"Stop talking about me as if I'm not here," the ferret complained. He tried to walk on his wounded paw. "Owww!" He was obviously in pain.

That snapped Emily back to reality. "We've got to get him to my mom. She can fix up his leg."

"No way—I am staying right here. I am *not* going anywAahHH!" The ferret screamed and leaped onto Emily's leg, grabbing at her shirt with his claws. Emily turned. Her heart began to pound. A great silver wolf stepped out of the shadows and walked to the dark-haired girl's side. It sat down and cocked its head at Emily. It was the wolf from the glade.

"Hello, healer."

Emily was stunned. Was that the *wolf*'s voice in her mind?

"Help, it's a mistwolf!" yelled the terrified ferret.

The girl was patting the wolf. "You know this person?"

"We had an adventure," the wolf replied.

"What?" The girl sounded hurt.

"Thank you for … whatever you did," Emily stammered, trying to pull the panicked ferret off by his good leg. "I think you, uh, might've saved the dogs and me."

"How can *you* hear her?" the other girl demanded angrily.

"I don't know," Emily whispered. "I just can."

The dark-haired girl raised her hands in frustration. "What's going on around here?"

"Good question," Emily answered, shaken. What *was* going on in these woods? Some weirdness that made her think animals could talk?

The other girl turned and bent close to the wolf. "I don't like this. I thought you only talked to me."

"This is unlike you, warrior," the wolf said.

"But it's *our* secret," she pleaded.

"She is a healer," the wolf replied calmly.

Emily was a little shaken by the wolf's words.

"Gahh! Stay away from it! It's a mistwolf!" the ferret screamed, poking his head out from behind Emily's arm.

"Stop whining, she's not going to eat you!" The dark-haired girl got to her feet, distracted from her anger and suspicion.

"I will leave until later," the wolf told her. *"The little traveler needs time."* Rising, the wolf wheeled about on her haunches and padded back into the woods.

"Smart wolf," Emily commented.

The other girl glared at her. "I don't know who you think you are, but these are *my* secrets."

"Whatever!" Emily felt like her circuits were overloaded. She couldn't take any more of this bizarre input. "I'm taking this ferret back to the clinic." "A ferret?!" The ferret was looking himself over in Emily's arms.

"Maybe my mom can figure out what it is," Emily continued.

"What do you mean, what it is?" The other girl moved closer.

Emily tried to stay calm. "Animals do not talk."

"Well, this one does. And all we need is your mom to tell everyone." The girl started pacing. She gazed in the direction where the wolf had disappeared, then looked pleadingly back to Emily. "People think this place is weird enough already!"

"You're just going to accept a ferret that talks?"

"Could you wait, at least?" the girl asked.

"For what?"

"Just wait, that's all ... to tell your mother. Until we can figure out what all this is about."

Emily stared at the girl she had only just met. She could tell that the girl cared deeply for these woods—and for the animals that lived here.

"Well, my mom can set its leg anyway." Cradling the ferret gently in her arms, she started walking away.

"It'd be faster if you go the other way."

Emily stopped. "What?"

The raven-haired girl sighed. "Come on, you'll just get lost," she said, dusting off the seat of her black jeans.

"Fine!"

Emily followed the girl and soon they were on a narrow dirt track, heading out of the preserve. The ferret lay still in the crook of Emily's arm, muttering incoherently.

"I'm Emily Fletcher," Emily offered.

"Adriane Charday."

"Hi, Adriane. Nice to meet you again."

"Yeah," Adriane said half-heartedly. "Uh ... same here."

" ... maybe it was the wrong portal," the ferret mumbled. "Maybe I should have gotten better directions ... maybe I should have just stayed home!"

"I didn't know there were wolves in this part of the country," Emily tried again.

"This *is* a wildlife preserve, you know," Adriane snapped. She caught herself and calmed down. "Her name is Stormbringer. She's a mistwolf."

"Mistwolves! What have I gotten myself into?" the ferret

whined.

"I've never heard of mistwolves," Emily said, trying to ignore the fact she was holding a talking ferret.

"Mistwovles are legendary, everyone's heard of them!" the ferret squirmed in Emily's arms.

"She's the last of her kind," Adriane said.

"How do you know that?"

"She told me," Adriane answered.

"That is so weird!"

"No weirder than the fact that *you* can hear her speak," Adriane retorted.

The girls looked at each other.

"Just what kinds of animals are on this preserve?" Emily asked incredulously.

"All kinds—supposedly. I haven't found any except for Storm … and the cat—and now this ferret."

"Adriane, I think the wolf saved me yesterday," Emily said in a soft voice. "I was about to be attacked by this … I don't know, animal-thing, I couldn't really see it clearly, but the wolf hid me in this mist … " she faltered. It still seemed so unbelievable.

"You think that thing attacked the cat?" Adriane asked

"I … don't know."

Adriane took a deep breath. "Look, I'm sorry I was such a jerk. I didn't want to share this with anyone. I've only known Storm for a few weeks, she's *so* amazing … "

"I understand." Emily nodded. "Not that I've got anyone to tell," she added under her breath.

Adriane heard her anyway. "What do you mean?"

"We just moved to Stonehill, my mom and me. I don't have any friends here."

"I should have stayed in the Misty Moors ... dumb Fairimental magic ... " the ferret complained as the girls walked on.

"Noisy, isn't he?" Adriane commented.

"Adriane, animals *don't* talk!"

"Before I met Storm I would've said the same thing."

"I've got to find that portal!" the ferret yelled out.

"What?" both girls asked in unison.

"Something is not right! I have to get back home!" the ferret exclaimed.

"Where do you come from?"

The ferret narrowed his eyes and looked around suspiciously "I'm not talking ... not saying another word."

"Good," Adriane said.

"Not a peep," added the ferret.

"Fine," said Emily.

"A ferret ... " the ferret moaned. "How revolting!"

"He must be delirious," Adriane said to Emily.

The girls made their way across the park grounds and into Emily's backyard. They entered the animal hospital through the back door.

The ferret looked around. "Wh-where am I?"

"At a place where we can take care of your leg," Emily said, depositing him on the examining table.

"I don't need to be taken care of," the ferret insisted. "I need to be changed out of this body! Gah! Wait till I get my hands on those Fairimentals!"

"Paws," Emily reminded him. "You have paws."

"What are Fairimentals?" Adriane asked.

"Uh-oh. Me and my big mouth," the ferret said,

beginning to back away. He regarded them with fear in his eyes. "How do I know you're not the enemy?"

"The enemy? What enemy?" Adriane asked.

"We're friends," Emily assured him. She heard footsteps approaching the room. "Ssshhh," she said suddenly. "Don't say a word! Just let my mother set your leg. She's a doctor."

The ferret sighed. "All right, all right. Just make it snappy. I've got to find that portal—"

"Quiet!"

The door opened and Carolyn came in, her face drawn and pale. She smiled at Emily. "Hi, Doc, what do you have there?"

"What's wrong, Mom?" Emily asked. Her heart skipped a beat. "Oh no! Not the cat?"

"No, a dog was found this morning near Arrowhead Park …"

"It didn't make it?" Emily asked.

Carolyn shook her head sadly. "Oh, hello again," she said, noticing Adriane. "Aren't you the girl who found the cat?"

Adriane nodded.

"She's doing fine, thanks to your quick thinking." Smiling, Emily's mom held out her hand. "I'm Carolyn Fletcher."

"Adriane Charday." Adriane shook her hand politely. "I found this ferret up on the preserve. Emily helped me free him from a trap."

"A trap!" Carolyn turned to Emily. "Didn't I did tell you to stay out of those woods? It's not safe up there!"

"I agree!" the ferret exclaimed.

Adriane clasped her hand over the ferret's mouth. "Shut

up!"

"What?" Carolyn said.

"Uh, wassup? With his paw, I mean." Keeping a hand over the ferret's mouth, Adriane stretched him out lengthwise.

Carolyn gently felt up and down both rear paws. "This doesn't look bad," she said. "No breaks, not even much of a wound. Lucky for him it wasn't a big trap."

Emily bent over the ferret. She looked at him, then at Adriane. "What the … " She peered at his injured paw. The leg was sound and straight! "Must have been the other leg … " she muttered, turning him over in Carolyn's hands.

Emily stared in astonishment. The ferret was practically healed! She was about to tell her mother that not thirty minutes ago his leg had been broken, but she caught Adriane glaring at her. Emily remained silent.

"You can handle this, Doc," Carolyn said, walking toward the recovery room. "Just clean the wound and bandage it."

"Okay, Mom," Emily said.

Adriane grabbed the ferret close to her face. "Listen, you —keep your mouth shut in front of other people!"

"I will do no such thing!" he said, crossing his paws and looking away.

"Oh, yes, you will," Emily insisted. "You want to be taken away and examined by a billion doctors and scientists?"

"Well … I … "

"And probed and dissected?" Adriane added.

"Gak!"

Adriane handed the ferret to Emily as Carolyn walked

back inside, drying her hands with a towel. Emily grabbed a bottle full of water and shoved it in the ferret's mouth, cradling him like a baby.

"Poor thing is thirsty," Adriane commented.

"Blurbbboo!"

"Completely dehydrated," Emily agreed.

"Foothpagg!"

Carolyn turned to Adriane. "So, Adriane, how is it that you were on the preserve?"

"My grandmother's the caretaker. I live with her there."

Emily gave Adriane a sharp glance. "Where are your parents?" she asked.

"Emily … " her mother said softly.

"I have parents." Adriane glared back at Emily. "They're artists, they travel a lot." She looked very uncomfortable.

Carolyn smiled. "Well, you're welcome here any time," she said.

"Mom?" Emily began. "That dog … " She faltered.

"What about it?" her mother prompted her.

"How did it … I mean, what killed it?"

Her mother sighed. "I'd have to say that whatever attacked the cat was the same thing that killed the dog." She headed for the door. "I've got to run to an appointment. I'll be home in time for dinner."

The moment Carolyn was out the door, Emily whirled on Adriane. "What's going on over there?"

"PhatoooiIEE!" The ferret leaped to the table and scampered away. "What are you trying to do, drown me?"

"What are you talking about?"

"You live there, you must know something. Or your grandmother does."

"No, she doesn't!" Adriane was horrified.

"Hurt animals are being found in those woods!"

Adriane blinked back tears. "You think *we're* doing something to hurt the animals? My gran loves animals!" Adriane started to pace. She whirled around to face Emily. "You're as bad as everyone else in this stupid town!" She stalked toward to door. "I'm outta here."

Emily ran after her. "Wait!"

Adriane stood there, arms crossed over her chest, glowering.

Emily felt ashamed. "I'm sorry. I just get so *mad*! I *hate* seeing animals hurt."

"Me, too," Adriane said quietly.

"I shouldn't have accused your grandma, but have you ever asked her what's going on?"

"I can't talk to her." Adriane raised her arms in frustration. "She's always saying weird stuff about spirits and giving me herbal roots and yucky charms."

"Yucky charms? They're magically delicious!" Emily exclaimed.

The girls broke out laughing.

"Aaaagh!" The high-pitched scream made them jump. It came from the adjoining room. They ran in—and found the cat standing on the makeshift bed straddling the ferret and looking at him as if he were a tasty treat.

"Help!" the ferret screamed.

The cat looked up. Seeing Emily, she backed off and crouched, still eyeing the ferret, a low growl rumbling from her chest. The ferret rolled out from under the cat's paws and fell on the floor with a thud. "This beast thinks I'm a rodent!"

"Ferrets are not rodents, more like weasels," Emily informed the ferret.

"That's comforting!"

She walked over to the cat. "This mean ol' ferret scare you?" She brushed her hand over the cat's back. Most of the bandages had been removed but the terrible scars remained. The cat nudged Emily with her head, then rubbed against her. The growl turned into a purr that sounded like a lawnmower.

"Glad to see you're getting your normal appetite back," Emily told her with a smile.

"Don't tell me she talks, too!" Adriane exclaimed incredulously.

"Not exactly ... I mean—this is so crazy! Animals *don't* talk!"

"Well, then," Adriane said, "what about him?" She jerked her thumb at the ferret, which was poking around the room, exploring curiously.

The ferret made his way to the side of a shiny metal cabinet. "Stupid thing thought I was a weasel." His reflection glared back at him and he shrieked.

"And what about Stormbringer?"

Emily's mind was whirling, trying to sort it all out. "I hear the wolf clearly—in my head. But the ferret actually talks out loud."

"What about the cat?" Adriane stroked the cat's head with gentle fingertips.

"She's ... like faint static. I can just barely make out a word here and there." Emily shook her head. "But how can we hear them at all?"

"I started hearing Storm when I found this." Adriane rummaged in her pocket and pulled out a shiny stone.

Shaped like a paw print, it was banded in gold, amber, and brown. "It's a wolf stone."

Emily's eyes went wide. "That is *so* weird."

"I kind of like it," Adriane said defensively.

Emily reached into her pocket and pulled out her own gemstone. "No, I mean, look at this."

Adriane stared in amazement. "Where did you find that?"

"In this glade on the preserve. I saw some birds and some ... weird deer."

"You saw animals there?" Adriane asked.

"Yeah," Emily said. She felt her pulse quicken at the memory of what had happened there. "Where did you find yours?" she asked.

"In the woods near a big field."

"I wonder if there are any more," Emily mused.

Adriane shrugged. "I don't know."

The sound of a loud purr distracted them. They looked over to see the ferret scratching the big cat under her chin. The cat's eyes were closed in pleasure.

"I'm really an elf, you know," the ferret was telling the cat.

The cat stretched and licked the ferret's head.

"Blah!"

"Emily, do you believe in magic?" Adriane asked.

Emily shook her head. "If you asked me that yesterday, I would have thought you were nuts. Now ... I don't know."

The front door of the clinic banged open, and Emily heard Kevin's familiar, clomping stride coming down the hall toward them.

Instinctively, both girls stuffed their stones into their

pockets. Emily went to the door and opened it. Kevin, holding a Fed-Ex envelope, came into the room. "Hey, Em," he said.

Then he saw Adriane behind her. "Oh, hey," he said to her.

"Hey, yourself," she replied.

"Yeah, whatever," he said, waving the envelope at Emily. "This came for your mom."

Emily looked at it. The return address was the University of Pennsylvania. Curiosity got the better of her and she snatched the envelope. "She's not here right now. I'll give it to her later, okay?"

Kevin frowned, but after a glance at Adriane, decided not to object. "I've got some shelves to stock," he said, backing out of the room. "See you later."

"Yeah." Adriane looked down.

Emily stood there, holding the package.

"The other kids around here don't like me much," Adriane said after Kevin was gone. "I'm used to it, though."

"They're just being jerks."

"So what is it?" Adriane nodded at the envelope.

"Lab report on the skin samples from the cat," Emily explained. After a moment's hesitation, she opened the envelope and read the report. Its contents made her heart sink.

"Listen to this: 'Results of testing are inconclusive … traces of toxin … recommend extreme caution … The area should be quarantined until further testing by agents from the Centers for Disease Control.'"

Adriane gasped. "Quarantined? They can't do that! Me and Gran live there!" She grabbed Emily's arm. "You have to hide that letter!"

"But it was sent to my mom. I shouldn't even have opened it."

"Emily, if they shut down the preserve, we'll have to move," Adriane pleaded. "I've only been there six months, but it's my home now. I can't move again!"

Emily thought for a moment. "Okay, I'll keep the letter hidden—for now. But if this radiation, or whatever it is, is not coming from the preserve, then where is it coming from?"

"I don't know." Adriane sprang up. "I've got to go tell Gran what's going on. If they close down the preserve, who'll protect the animals?"

The question echoed in Emily's mind. "I'll come with you." She grabbed the ferret, who was busy examining his reflection. "I think we'd better take you with us, before somebody hears you talking."

"What's wrong with me talking?" he asked, sounding insulted.

"Around here," Emily told him, "ferrets don't talk."

"I am not a ferret. I am an elf."

"Yeah, and I'm Dr. Doolittle," Emily said.

"I'm an elf!" he insisted again. "My name is Ozymandias. You can call me Ozzie." He smiled a ferret smile.

Adriane stared at him. "We need to make a pact," she turned to Emily. "To keep all this secret—at least for now."

"Okay."

The two girls held out their hands. As they shook, a furry paw came down and sealed their pact.

6

EMILY FOLLOWED ADRIANE across the park and over a small hill that put them right on the main road to Ravenswood Wildlife Preserve. Ozzie rode comfortably in Emily's backpack. His head poked out of the top, snout covered with crumbs from a power bar he'd found inside.

"Okay, Mr. Ozzie the Talking Ferret, spill it." Adriane smacked the side of the backpack.

"Spoof!" Ozzie spit out a mouthful of power bar. "What-what-what?"

"Where did you come from?" she asked.

"How did you get here?" Emily added, swinging the pack around to rest against her chest.

"How come you can talk?" Adriane demanded.

"Stop, you're making me dizzy! One minute I was there, then I fell through the portal to here. I'm an elf. Well, I *was* an elf. Now look at me. I'm a furry beast with paws and *fleas*!"

He tried to scratch his back. Emily reached into the pack and scratched it for him.

"A little to the right—ooooh, good one."

They passed through the iron gates of the preserve and headed down the main road.

"What's a portal?" Emily asked.

"It's a … you know … a portal," Ozzie said.

"No, we don't know," said Adriane.

"A doorway between worlds," Ozzie explained. "I fell through one and ended up here."

"And where did you come from Alice … Wonderland?" Adriane asked, rolling her dark eyes.

"Ozzie! And I came from *my* world!"

Adriane was starting to get impatient. "Listen, ferret face … " She leaned toward him.

"Gak!" Ozzie dove back into the pack.

Emily gave Adriane a stern look. "Does your world have a name?" she asked Ozzie.

"Aldenmor," Ozzie squeaked from inside the pack.

"What are Fairimentals?" Emily asked.

Ozzie popped his head back out. "Don't you know *anything*? They're magic—the really powerful stuff."

"What do the Fairimentals want?" Emily asked.

"They are looking for … something."

The girls stopped and both looked at the ferret. "What?"

"Mages," Ozzie whispered. "Magic users."

"Magic? You sure fell down the wrong rabbit hole, Alice." Adriane laughed and smacked the backpack again.

"It's Ozzie!"

The road ended at the circular drive in front of the manor house. Emily stared in awe at the old architectural monstrosity. Close up, it seemed spookier than ever, but at the same time, it looked inviting, full of secrets waiting to be revealed.

"You actually live here?" Emily walked over and peered in the sidelight windows that framed the enormous wooden front door. Ozzie clambered out of her backpack and leaped to the ground.

"No, we live in a cottage around the back," Adriane explained.

"I wonder what it's like inside," Emily murmured, burning with curiosity.

"Most of the place is locked up," Adriane told her. "But it has a ton of rooms and an old library up top."

"That sounds cool." Emily stepped back and looked at the huge brass door knocker. It was shaped like the head of a lion. "Kevin told me they used to have tours here."

"Yeah, that was a long time ago."

"So what do you think happened to Mr. Gardener?" Emily asked.

"I don't know. He just disappeared."

"I hope he ended up better than I did," Ozzie commented.

A sudden scuffling noise from inside the house made them jump.

"Maybe he's still inside," Emily said, uncertainly.

"No way," Adriane scoffed.

"Should we knock?" Emily pressed on the door—it was open. She glanced at Adriane with a look of surprise, then pushed the door in all the way. The hinges squealed softly.

The girls peered in. Ozzie craned his head around Emily's legs to get a look for himself. A wide hallway ran from the front door to an open foyer filled with couches, tables, and chairs. The girls were careful to leave the door open behind them. In silence, they edged forward, into the foyer. Emily let out a loud breath.

"Wow! Look at this place!"

Paintings hung on the walls: animals in beautiful garden settings; the mansion itself, in all its early glory; gardens filled with deer, peacocks—even lions and tigers!

"These are amazing!" Emily stopped in front of a large painting of a man surrounded by three white tigers. "Who's that?" she asked.

Adriane glanced up. "That's Mr. Gardener."

Creeeaaakkk—thud!

The front door had closed. The girls whirled around as a figure stepped out from a column of dusty sunlight.

"I see you've made some new friends, Little Bird."

It was an old woman. She had dark wrinkled skin, and piercing dark eyes like Adriane's. A long white braid hung over her shoulder in sharp contrast to her forest green ankle-length dress. Her arms jingled with silver and turquoise bracelets.

"Gran, we were just looking for you," Adriane exclaimed. "This is Emily ... and this is, um ... "

Ozzie stood beside Emily, arms crossed, tapping one paw on the floor. He didn't say a word.

Gran bowed to him. "Welcome, Woodland Spirit," she said. Ozzie's eyes widened.

Then Gran turned and looked Emily up and down with a piercing gaze. "Come here, child. I don't bite."

Emily shuddered. Kevin had said this woman was a witch. She knew that had to be nonsense, but staring at the old woman now, she suddenly wasn't so sure. She glanced uncertainly at Adriane, who just rolled her eyes.

Gran reached out and touched Emily's cheek with gentle fingers. "You are a special one, child."

"Thank you ... I think."

Gran chuckled. "It is good to see Little Bird with friends. My name is Nakoda, but you can call me Gran."

"These pictures ... " Emily asked. "Do all those animals live here, on the preserve?"

"At one time or another," Gran replied. "I have been with Mr. Gardener for over forty-five years now."

"Where *is* Mr. Gardener?" Emily asked.

"Oh, I'm sure he's on important business."

"Something to do with animals?" Emily pressed.

"Most probably. He's quite the animal expert."

"My mom's a vet. We love animals."

"I can tell. Come, its so dusty here, why don't we go to our house."

The girls followed Gran out the front door. Emily leaned in to whisper to Adriane. "How come she calls you Little Bird?"

"It's my Indian name—she gave it to me. She's Bird Woman, so ... I'm stuck with it, until I find my own." Adriane paused, looking uncomfortable.

Emily shrugged. "My mom calls me 'Doc.' I don't mind."

"Yeah, real cute. Hey, you don't have to stay if you don't want—it's okay."

"Are you kidding? This place is so cool!"

The caretaker's cottage was off to the left of the main house, down a cobblestone path and through a grove of pines. The cottage was more like a lodge, with dark wooden beams making geometric patterns against a white plaster background. The girls and Ozzie followed Gran down a narrow hallway into a cozy, old-fashioned kitchen in the back of the house. It was bright and cheery. Crystals hung in the windows, catching the sunlight and casting rainbows on the walls. Gran poured some lemonade for the girls.

"Please, sit, eat," she said, gesturing to the wooden dining table off to the side of the room.

The girls sat down and Ozzie sniffed around the table. Suddenly famished, Emily took a cookie from the serving plate on the table. It was moist and delicious. Ozzie grabbed two cookies and ran off with them. Adriane sat without eating.

"Gran, we have to talk," she said. "About the animals."

"I know," Gran replied.

"What's happening to them?" Emily asked, trying not to sound accusing.

Gran looked sad. "I don't know, Emily. This place has always been a safe haven for animals. But something has changed."

"Gran," Adriane said, "people are going to come and shut the place down. Maybe worse … "

"I know, Little Bird. The mayor's office called earlier, requesting my presence at a town meeting tomorrow night. Animals are being hurt, and people are frightened."

"But they can't shut Ravenswood down!" Adriane protested. "It's our home!"

"Yes, this is our home and Mr. Gardener's, and home to many animals," her grandmother agreed.

Adriane stood up, eyes sparking. "We have to fight this!"

"Ah, Little Bird, you are so full of fire. Sometimes patience is the road to follow."

"But we have to *do* something!" Adriane pleaded.

"Have faith, Little Bird," Gran said calmly.

Emily and Adriane exchanged glances. Then Adriane seemed to come to some internal decision. She sat back down.

"Look, Gran," she said, pulling her stone out of her pocket. She held it out to show her grandmother.

"I found one, too," Emily said, holding out her stone.

Gran's eyebrows rose as she studied the stones. "Where did you get these?"

"We found them in the woods," Adriane told her.

"Keep these very safe," Gran said. "Crystals and gemstones are often charged with energy. They may hold strong magic."

The girls looked at each other.

"Magic?" Emily repeated.

Ozzie popped his head up by the side of the table.

"But the stones don't actually *do* anything." Emily turned to Adriane. "At least, mine doesn't."

"Sometimes that which seems to do nothing can have great effect," Gran explained. "A tiny pebble, thrown into a quiet pond, makes one ripple, then another, then a whole wave of ripples that spread in ever-growing circles."

"English please, Gran," Adriane said.

"There is much to learn about magic, Little Bird. Perhaps the obvious is not always the answer."

A furry paw stretched across the table, followed by a long furry body. "Delightmmphul," Ozzie mumbled, stuffing another cookie into his mouth.

The girls stared at the ferret. They stared down at their sparkling gems. They looked back at Ozzie.

"Whaaa?" Ozzie demanded around a mouthful of cookie. "Whaa I do?"

Gran didn't seem to notice. "I have work to do," she said, getting up. "You two—three—stay and eat." She walked out the kitchen door.

"I really like this house," Emily said after Gran had left the room.

Adriane jumped up. "Want to see my room?"

"Sure."

Emily got up and followed Adriane, leaving the ferret to his feast. "Don't eat too much," she called back to him. "You'll get a tummy ache."

"bUrrp," Ozzie replied.

Adriane's room was an explosion of color. Bright yellow paint peeked out in the spaces between the patchwork of posters on the walls; the ceiling was dark blue with constellations of glow-in-the-dark stars. Emily studied the posters. Rock bands, mountain climbers high above the clouds, Motocross bikers careening down dirt trails, snow boarders shooting sprays of white snow … She hardly knew Adriane, but she never would have pegged her for the type to have a room like this!

She turned around full circle, taking it all in. "It's fantastic!"

"Thanks." Adriane was much more animated in her own space. She leapt over the bed to rummage through the shelves by her stereo. "You like Smash Fish?" she asked over her shoulder.

"I've never eaten it. Any good?"

"Ha! It's a band. Here, listen to this." Crunching music blared out of two tower speakers. Two smaller satellite speakers hung from the opposite corners, creating a surround-sound effect. The music was a little harsher than what Emily was used to, but it was catchy, with a strong melody. She noticed a red electric guitar leaning against a wall. "Is that yours?" she asked.

"Yup!" Adriane bounced over to the guitar and picked it up. "Sweet, huh?"

"I guess."

Adriane ran her hands over the polished red body. "A real Fender Strat!" She strummed across the strings. "I've got this cool practice amp, too," she said, indicating a small box on the floor. "Check it out!"

The girls laughed as Adriane rocked out with the music.

"What is that horrible sound?" Ozzie stood in the doorway, paws over his ears.

"It's rock 'n' roll, Ozzie," Adriane said. "Real magic!"

Ozzie's eyes widened. "Ah, so this is magic in your world. It's so noisy!"

Adriane turned down the volume on the stereo and set her guitar gently against the dresser.

"Ozzie," Emily said, "we don't *have* magic here."

"I knew I fell in the wrong portal." Ozzie jumped on the bed and flopped over a large pillow. "Ooh, I just want to go home."

"So tell us, what's the magic like where you come from?" Adriane asked.

Ozzie stretched over the pillow. "Well, there's not much left. That's why the Fairimentals sent me here. To get help."

"Why do they need help?" Emily asked.

"Our world is in danger," he said. "There's something called the Black Fire. It's poisoning everything."

"Including animals?" Adriane looked to Emily.

"I suppose so. I was told it's the result of horrible dark magic."

"Tell us more about Fairimentals," Emily prompted.

"They're forces of nature and they protect the good magic of Aldenmor. I'm no expert but all magic is fueled by nature—air, water, earth, and fire."

"Sounds confusing," Adriane said.

Ozzie sighed. "*You're* confused? The Fairimentals sent me to find three human mages who can help us, but there's no magic here and I haven't met any mages—only you." He flopped over on his back. "*And* I'm a ferret!"

For some reason, Emily flashed on the bizarre twirling bits of leaves and dirt she had seen in the glade. "What do Fairimentals look like?" she asked.

But Ozzie had fallen asleep. Emily sat back, leaning against the wall. Then she noticed several objects hanging over Adriane's bed. They were round wooden hoops, with a variety of colorful strings and cords threaded across them, like a spiderweb. Gemstones were woven amid the strands, and feathers hung from the bottom.

"What are those?" she asked Adriane.

"Dreamcatchers," Adriane told her. "Gran hung them. She says they're a web of protection. They're supposed to catch bad dreams and let the good ones in through the center hole. The energy of the gemstones strengthens the good dreams."

"Like a barrier between two worlds," Emily said in a hushed voice.

"Emily," Adriane said hesitantly. "What if Ozzie really does come from another world?"

"So now we're also supposed to believe in magical worlds, too!" Emily shook her head.

Adriane stared at her. "After what's happened here—after what you've seen—can you sit there and tell me it's not possible?"

"I don't know," Emily had to admit. "There's so much weird stuff going on, I don't know what's possible."

Adriane was silent. She gazed at the dreamcatchers. A slight smile played across her lips. "You know what might be cool?" Her jet-black eyes flashed. "What if we took the stones *we* found and weave them into … "

"Dreamcatchers?" Emily guessed, intrigued.

"Better. Power bracelets," Adriane responded.

Emily was into it. "Sorta like making our own web of … "

"Protection." They'd said it together.

A few minutes later, the girls sat cross-legged on the floor amid a pile of rawhide strips, satin, and lanyard. Adriane had the idea to combine the colored lanyard and black satin string, and Emily shared some knots she knew. It took some trial and error to find a way to hold their stones securely, but at last they each had a very cool new bracelet.

Adriane held her arm out and turned her wrist this way and that. "Not bad," she said admiringly.

Emily stood up and stretched her legs. Her gaze settled on a framed photograph of a handsome couple.

Adriane saw her looking and took the photograph down. "My mom and dad. They're artists. They do these 'performance art' and sculpture exhibits. Pretty weird, huh?"

"How come you live with your grandmother?" Emily asked.

Adriane shrugged. "They left to go on a world tour. So they dumped me here in a nice *stable* environment for a change. They say they're going to settle in upstate New York when they get back but I've never been in the same school more than a year, sometimes less."

"My dad lives in Seattle. We e-mail each other a lot," Emily said.

"At least you talk to him. My parents send me postcards … sometimes."

Emily couldn't imagine being so out of touch with your own parents.

"So, you've been here six months, right?" Emily said, not wanting to intrude further. "That means you've been to school … "

"Middle school." Adriane snorted. "The way some kids act, you'd think it was Stonehill Academy."

"There must be some kids you like?" But Emily remembered the girls in the park.

Adriane shrugged. "Friends are overrated."

Emily blinked. "You can't mean that."

Adriane's silence told her she meant exactly that.

A pang of homesickness swept over Emily. She'd always had friends she totally connected with.

She turned around to face Adriane. "What do you think is going to happen at the meeting tomorrow night?"

"They'll probably kick me and Gran out of here." Adriane began to pace back and forth. "Then they're gonna send in the Army to kill all the animals. Then they'll cut down all the trees and make a golf course or something!"

Emily laughed, not knowing if Adriane was joking or not. "That's a bit extreme, don't you think?"

"You saw the letter. Quarantine! How extreme is that?"

"What can we do?" Emily asked, feeling a familiar wave of helplessness.

"If we can prove there really *are* rare animals here, they'd *have* to leave Ravenswood alone! That glade where you found your stone—do you think you could find that place again?" Adriane asked.

"It's right behind the Rocking Stone."

Adriane stopped. "There's nothing there but woods."

"No, that's where I saw it. I was going back there when I ran into you and Ozzie."

"We need to find that glade! Can you get away tomorrow?" Adriane asked.

"As long as I get my chores done … which reminds me, I should get back."

"What should we do about *him*?" Adriane jerked her thumb in the direction of the snoring ferret.

"I'll take him with me." Emily gently scooped the ferret up and deposited him in her backpack.

"Mommy, I don't want to ride the flobbin," Ozzie mumbled, sleepily.

Adriane shrugged. "Elves! Come on, I'll walk you and Alice up to the main road."

Outside, the western sky was awash with orange and purple, tingeing the forest with a magical glow. From out of nowhere, Stormbringer appeared by Adriane's side and joined the girls as they made their way along the road. The wolf was silent and Emily had to remind herself that Storm wasn't just Adriane's pet dog, jogging along beside them. When they reached the edge of the park grounds, the girls stopped.

"Okay, tomorrow we'll search the woods and see if we can find the animals," Adriane said.

"We're going to have to be really careful."

"I'm not afraid," Adriane boasted. "Are you?"

"I grew up hiking in the Colorado Mountains, where

plenty of wild animals roam—I'm not afraid." Emily tried to sound as brave as she could.

"You know," Adriane said, "there's an Iroquois story that says if two people wear the same bracelet, it means they're linked, joined."

"Like … friends?" Emily smiled and raised her bracelet.

Adriane grimaced. Then a small smile escaped her lips. She held her braceleted arm next to Emily's. The two gems sparkled in the fading sun.

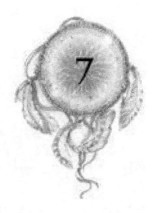

7

THE NEXT MORNING, Emily was up early. She dressed quickly, pulling on shorts and an aqua T-shirt. Sliding on her hiking boots, she ran downstairs to check on the cat. Her remaining bandages looked clean and dry—no more seepage through the white gauze, no unnatural glow evident at all—and she actually ate all the canned food Emily gave her.

Emily went to the Pet Palace and fed the dogs, then returned to the house, where she fetched Ozzie from her room. He was still sleeping on the big fluffy pillow she'd given him for a bed.

As she slipped him into her backpack, he opened his eyes. "Hey, what're you doing?"

"Rise and shine, we're off to see the wizard."

"Really? That's great news!"

Emily shook her head as she bounced down the stairs. "You are one wacky ferret."

"Thank you."

Carolyn was sitting in the kitchen eating a grapefruit and making notes in her scheduling book.

"Hey, Mom." Emily opened the refrigerator and grabbed

the orange juice. "I'm going over to Adriane's, okay?"

"Chores done?"

Emily smiled. "Yup. And the cat's doing much better, too."

Carolyn smiled. "That's great, Doc. But wouldn't it be better if Adriane came here?"

"Why?" Emily gulped down her juice while she waited for an English muffin to toast.

"I'm not happy about you going into those woods."

"Mom! Adriane lives in a house, not in the woods!" She left out the fact that once she was at Adriane's house, she was, technically, already in the woods. She lathered her breakfast with jam and handed a piece to Ozzie.

"Strawberry! Yumm!"

Carolyn looked over. Emily and Ozzie both smiled back.

EMILY MADE HER way across the park and up the road to the preserve. The morning air held a faint crispness that reminded her summer was fading. She sighed, thinking of what September would bring: more changes.

Ozzie was rummaging around in her backpack.

"Stop fidgeting," she told him.

"Where's the oatmeal ones?"

"They're in there."

Ozzie stuck his head out. "Can this wizard help us find the portal?"

"I was kidding about the wizard."

"Oh." Ozzie leaned out of the pack, clearly depressed. "I'll never get home, will I?"

"Maybe *we* can help you."

He perked up. "You'd help me?"

"Of course I would, and Adriane would, too"

"You know, if I have to be stuck here, I'm glad it's with you."

Emily smiled.

They found Adriane outside the cottage, brushing the mistwolf's coat to a shiny luster. Stormbringer's eyes were closed in pleasure, but she opened them when Emily and Ozzie arrived.

"Morning," Adriane said with a smile as she glided the brush over the wolf's back. She had on hiking boots, black T-shirt and jeans, and a baseball cap with the words NO FEAR embroidered on it.

"Hey!" Emily returned. She looked at the wolf. "Hi, Stormbringer!"

"Hello, healer. Hello, traveler," the wolf replied, nodding to Ozzie.

"Why do you call me 'healer?'" Emily asked.

"That is what you do," the wolf replied.

"Just don't call me breakfast!" Ozzie scrambled down Emily's side to the ground.

"I have already eaten," the wolf assured him. She looked as if she were grinning. *"It was a—"*

"Gah! Don't tell me—I don't want to know!" Ozzie put his paws over his ears.

Adriane knelt and unrolled a large scroll. "Check this out. It's a map of the preserve. I took it off the wall in the foyer."

The girls spread the map on the ground and crouched over it. Ozzie joined them.

"It's old, but the basic layout of the preserve is still the same," Adriane said. "So ... I say we start here up at the north quadrant and follow this trail. It winds down here to the Rocking Stone."

"I don't see the glade near the stone," Emily observed.

"It's not on the map."

"I fell out in a big, open area," Ozzie offered, walking out onto the map to study it.

"Looking for the rabbit hole, Alice?" Adriane asked the ferret.

"I am not a rabbit." Ozzie looked himself over just to make sure.

"Do you have any idea how we can find it?" Emily asked him.

"I don't know, but it's magic. Magic attracts magic—I know that much," he replied.

"We don't have any magic," Emily reminded him.

"Gran said these stones hold magic." Adriane held up her wrist. Sunlight reflected off the gold and amber jewel.

Adriane rolled up the map, stood, and slung her olive-green backpack over her shoulder. "Let's move out!"

Emily followed Adriane across the wide lawn in back of the manor. A garden of hedges and flowers lay just beyond the green; the hedges were planted in geometric patterns with pathways in between, like a maze. Near the entrance stood a large stone fountain in the shape of a mermaid. She held a beautiful carved urn over her head and water poured from it to splash off her up-curved tail into the round basin below.

"This place is just so amazing," Emily breathed.

"C'mon, slowpokes!" Adriane had ducked through an opening in the trees at the edge of the lawn. Emily quickened her steps to catch up. They found themselves on a trail winding through a section of open woodlands. Narrow swaths of meadow separated clusters of trees and bushes. Stormbringer trotted on ahead, fading from view among the tall feathery grasses and wildflowers.

"I feel like I'm on a safari!" Emily exclaimed. The girls crossed a small stream and entered a section of forest thick with tall junipers and furs.

Suddenly Adriane stopped and looked around. "Hold up," she said.

Emily heard a rustling of leaves and the patter of approaching hoofbeats. "Over there!" She pointed through the trees.

The most amazing creatures came bounding through the woods. They looked like deer, but with long ears and green stripes.

"What *are* those?" Adriane whispered.

"They're like the animals I saw in the glade. Maybe some kind of zebra?" Emily guessed.

"Jeeran," Ozzie simply stated.

The girls looked at him.

"What?" Emily asked incredulously.

"Jeeran, herdbeasts found in the hills of the Moorgroves. I've seen lots of them. They're fast and jump really high."

"Don't tell me they come from your world, too?" Adriane asked.

"Okay."

"Okay, what?" Emily asked.

"Okay, I won't tell you," Ozzie replied.

"Wherever they came from, they're here now," Adriane laughed. "Come on, this is wild!"

The girls ran through the woods and came to a wide-open field, but the strange animals were too swift, and the field was empty. Adriane kicked the dirt.

"Look, there's the Rocking Stone!" Emily pointed to where the jagged peak rose above the trees in the distance.

Adriane pulled the map from her backpack and studied it. "We can pick up the trail on the other side."

They started across the open field. The tall grass brushed against their legs. The air smelled sweet as soft particles blew around them.

"Hey! Look at you—you're sparkling!" Adriane said.

Emily looked down at her arms and saw that they were, indeed, sparkling. Her legs looked like they were covered in tiny glittering lights. Then she saw them. "It's the rainbow flowers!" she exclaimed. All through the grassy expanse, they were sending tiny bursts of color into the air.

"That is *so* cool!" Adriane exclaimed, spinning around like a dancer.

"Your hair is all sparkly," Emily laughed. Rainbow twinkles were catching on Adriane's long, dark hair.

Ozzie hopped out of Emily's pack and started nosing around in the flowers. "Magic seeds. This is good, very good."

"What are you talking about, Jack?" Adriane asked him, grinning. "They're going to grow into beanstalks?"

"Jack?" Ozzie looked around. Then he nosed a flower again. "Can't you feel it? It's fairy magic!"

"These flowers were all over that glade," Emily said. "Right before … " Her voice trailed off. "Where's Storm?"

"Off somewhere. She has a mind of her own." Adriane was crouched low, studying something in the dirt. "There are animals around here somewhere," she announced.

"What did you find?" Ozzie nosed his way over to look. "BLAH! That's disgusting!"

"Quiet, Alice, it's just animal droppings."

There was a rustling in the grass. The three turned together. A jeeran was standing there watching them, not fifteen yards away. Soft green-striped fur rustled as it breathed. Big purple eyes blinked at the girls.

"Wow. I've never seen anything like that," Emily whispered.

"It's so amazing. What do we do? Like, hello we come in peace?" asked Adriane.

"Might work," Emily replied.

Emily started walking slowly towards the animal. The jeeran tensed but stood still as Emily approached. It stood as high as Emily's nose. She stepped closer, hand reaching out. Ever so slowly, her finger made contact with the animal's forehead and it blinked its eyes, pulling its head back to sniff her fingers. Emily smiled and ran her hand over the animal's mane. The fur felt so soft and silky. Emily broke out in a grin. She turned to face the others.

"It likes me."

Bang!

The sound of gunfire split the air. Ozzie screamed. The jeeran bolted.

"Guns!" Emily exclaimed. "Someone's shooting!"

"Over that hill!" Adriane pointed.

Ozzie dived into Emily's backpack. "They don't hunt ferrets in this world, do they?" he squeaked.

"They shouldn't be hunting here at all!" Adriane exclaimed angrily. She ran up the hill. Emily and Ozzie followed.

On the other side of the hill, three hunters were creeping across the grass. One of the men had his rifle raised. The other two were holding a huge net between them. They were moving slowly toward the most bizarre creature Emily had ever seen.

"What the—!" Ozzie scampered to Emily's shoulder to get a better look.

"Is *that* the monster?" Adriane asked.

"That's no monster!" Ozzie exclaimed. "I'd recognize that purple furball anywhere!"

As they watched, the hunters crept slowly toward the huge creature, but unlike other animals, this one didn't seem to have a sense of danger. It didn't move. It just sat.

Ozzie was getting more agitated. "That's Phelonius!" He dug his claws into Emily's scalp.

"Ouch! Calm down, Ozzie!" Emily pulled him off her head.

"We've got to help him!" Ozzie wriggled out of her arms and leaped to the ground.

The men were shaking their heads and gesturing toward each other. Then the man with the rifle pointed it at the sky. *Bang!* The creature still didn't move. The man lowered his gun and moved forward slowly.

"We can't let them capture Phel!" Ozzie insisted.

Emily looked at Adriane.

"I don't know, it's a talking ferret, maybe they're all crazy," Adriane offered.

"It's a creature of magic!" Ozzie yelled

"And it's not dangerous?" Adriane asked.

"Nooo!" Ozzie was very frazzled. "You've got to do something!" he urged the girls.

Emily nodded her head at Adriane. "All right."

Adriane straightened her shoulders. "Okay, I'll distract those hunters, while you and Alice see if you can move that

… thing … out of here."

"Be careful," Emily said, crouching low in the tall grass.

"You, too." Adriane took a deep breath and confidently walked down the hill. "Hey!"

Startled, all three hunters whirled to face her.

"It's a kid!" one of them said. "Go on home, it's not safe around here."

Undaunted, Adriane continued until she was right next to them. "This is a wildlife preserve," she said. "Didn't you see the signs? They say 'No hunting.'"

"Who are you?" the rifle-holder asked.

"I'm Adriane Charday. I live at Ravenswood Manor."

"We don't have to listen to a kid," one of the net-holding men said.

Their backs were to the creature—and to Emily. She seized the moment. "Let's go," she said to Ozzie. She dashed into the field and skidded to a stop right in front of the purple giant. Ozzie was running so fast he hit the creature's belly and bounced back off. The thing was enormous, easily eight feet tall. It sat motionless in the grass, surrounded by a ring of rainbow puff flowers. Deep purple fur shimmered in the sunlight. Emily stared in wonder. It looked sort of like a cross between a great bear and Humpty Dumpty. Its giant eyes were shut. A think line for a mouth ran across its face and it had no neck. Ozzie scrambled up the huge beast and looked into its face. "Phelonius! It's me! Ozymandius!"

The creature just sat, eyes closed, still as a statue.

"Maybe he's been tranquilized," Emily whispered.

"No, no," the ferret said quickly. "He can't be tranquilized. That's absurd!"

"You have no right bringing rifles onto private property!" Adriane yelled in the distance.

"This preserve has no right harboring killer grizzlies," one of the men countered.

"That's no grizzly! It's a rare ... um, panda from China ... and it's worth a million dollars! If anything happens to it, you'd be responsible!"

"I don't care what it is, we're bringing it in!" the hunter threatened.

Emily studied the creature. She felt oddly drawn to him. She realized she should probably be scared—but she wasn't. She ran her hand over his smooth fur and felt a wave of calm wash over her. Light caught her eye, and she looked down to see her gem pulse a soft aqua blue. She took a deep breath.

"What are you?" she asked.

"He's a fairy creature." Ozzie had resorted to kicking the giant. "Wake up, you big thing!"

Looking past the creature, Emily saw that the field fell away into a shallow gully. "Maybe we can roll him down into that gully." She placed her hands on the creature and pushed. "Come on, Ozzie, help me!"

The creature put up no resistance as he started to tilt over. Despite his girth, he felt as light as air.

"What?" Ozzie cried. "That's ridiculous, you can't roll—aaaahhhhh!"

In a cloud of rainbow dust, the giant furball starting rolling down the hill, the shrieking ferret hanging on.

"What was that?" asked one of the hunters.

"If you harm that panda, you're all going to be in big trouble!" Adriane yelled.

"Get out of our way!"

The huge creature rolled to a stop in the gully, sitting upright. Keeping her head down, Emily quickly crawled back to peer across the field. She saw the man with the rifle start to shove past Adriane.

Suddenly he stopped. "Hey, where did it go?"

Watching Adriane point to the trees in the direction opposite the gully, Emily noticed an opalescent glow at her friend's wrist. The section of woods that Adriane was pointing to rustled and shook, as if disturbed by something passing through.

"Look over there!" a hunter cried. "It's in those trees!"

The hunter with the rifle moved off in the direction of the sounds. "Come on!"

For a moment, Adriane looked stunned. Then she seemed to collect herself and yelled after them. "And stay off this property!"

8

THE ENORMOUS CREATURE sat like a giant Buddha, unaffected by anything that had happened.

Adriane came sliding into the gully. "That was *so* weird!" she exclaimed breathlessly.

"How did you do that?" Emily asked, wide eyed.

"I don't know," Adriane said slowly. "I was so focused on doing something to distract the hunters. Then I saw the trees and reached for them … it was intense, it felt like I was pushing through water."

"I saw your stone glow," Emily said.

Adriane glanced at her bracelet. The paw shaped stone looked perfectly normal. "I pushed harder, in my head, and my stone flashed and then the trees across the field started to shake and move!"

Emily peered at her own gemstone. "Do you think these are really magic stones?"

"Memerrmeemee!"

Adriane looked around. "Where's Alice?"

"Ozzie!" Emily stood up quickly. "Where are you?"

"MmurrRRMMppphh!"

83

Emily circled the purple creature. "Ozzie?"

"Mm hmm ... !"

She put her hands on the giant. His fur felt warm and soft. "Help me move him."

Adriane got up and pushed alongside Emily. Two gigantic eyes opened and blinked. They were deep reservoirs of calm and gentleness. He blinked again.

"Please, could you move just a little?" Emily tried. "Our friend seems to be caught under you."

The purple giant seemed to search Emily's face. She felt overwhelmed by a sadness so deep that tears welled in her eyes. But the feeling passed in a flash and her hands fell away from the creature's side as he lumbered to his feet.

"Gah!" Ozzie sputtered.

Emily reached down to peel Ozzie off the ground. "Are you all right?"

"No! I'm all flattened out!" The ferret shook dust off himself and kicked the big creature. "What are you trying to do, squish me?"

The huge beast just blinked down at Ozzie. Then silently, he turned and started to walk away.

"Hey, come back here!" Ozzie yelled. He ran and grabbed hold of the creature's leg, then scampered all the way up to his shoulder.

"We'd better follow him until we're sure those hunters are really gone," Emily said.

The girls ran to catch up as the purple giant entered the woods. He moved silently forward as if gliding on air, trailing a colorful wake of rainbow flowers behind him.

"So that's where the flowers are coming from!" Emily exclaimed.

"Phelonious, am I glad to see you! I thought I was sent to the wrong place!" Ozzie gestured wildly with his arms as he chattered into the great beast's ear. "I ended up in this strange body—what were those Fairimentals thinking? Look, I'm a weasel!!!" he wailed.

A flash of color moved through the trees behind them. Emily grabbed Adriane's arm. "Did you see that?"

"See what?" Adriane stopped to look. In the stillness, they heard rustling and the patter of hoofbeats. Suddenly a herd of jeeran burst through the brush, bounding through the trees.

Adriane whirled around. "Look, there's more!"

Behind the jeeran, a group of strange duck-like birds appeared. They were goofy-looking, with silver bills and webbed feet too big for their bodies. One of them waddled right up to Emily. It cocked its head up at her, but made no threatening moves.

"Hello," Emily said.

"Hello yourself," it responded. It spoke out loud, its rubbery beak moving weirdly to shape the words. "Are you a mage?"

"Mage? No, I'm a girl."

"A warlock, then?" it persisted.

"We're not warlocks," Adriane said.

The creature thought for a moment. "All right then." It waddled past them, herding the others along the trail of rainbow flowers left behind by the purple giant Ozzie called Phelonius.

Following the parade of animals, the girls made their way around a mass of dense thickets. Phelonius was entering the natural archway that led to the Rocking Stone.

"This is it!" Adriane exclaimed. "The glade must be on

85

the other side!"

Emily hung back, suddenly overwhelmed by the reality of being back here again.

"C'mon!" Adriane called.

Reluctantly Emily followed, hoping the glade really *was* there. They skirted the immense boulder—and stopped.

"Wow." Adriane stopped, awestruck. "This is amazing!"

The glade was just as awesome as Emily remembered. The slender boughs of the weeping willows touched the pond, sending cascading ripples through the water's reflection of the sky. The ground was a flower-carpet of rainbow colors. Sparkling sunlight glinted off the turquoise wing of a bird perched on the arching bridge.

"Wow ... " Adriane breathed, looking around. "I can't believe this was here and I never knew it."

Phelonius was settling his great bulk beside an enormous tree. Stormbringer padded out from the far trees and walked over to him, lowering her head, her ears, and her tail in a wolfish bow. Emily caught brief glimpses of animals huddled together.

The ferret raced over to the girls.

"Ozzie, what is he doing here?" Emily asked, looking at the purple creature.

"I don't know yet. He's not talking."

"An animal that *doesn't* talk—what a concept," Adriane remarked.

"Phel is not an animal," Ozzie said. "Come and say hello."

Emily and Adriane followed Ozzie over to Phel. The glade was still. A brightly colored bird darted over the water and zipped past. Emily blinked. It looked like a tiny dragon, with wings! It was gone before she could be sure. She looked around and felt surrounded by animals. They stood at the outskirts of the glade waiting—but for what?

"This is Emily and Adriane," Ozzie said. "They're girls, but they seem to have a talent for magic." He sat back, pleased with himself.

"Hello," Emily said shyly.

"Hi," Adriane said.

Phelonius blinked, and Emily felt a wave of warmth and love pour over her.

"What kind of creature is he exactly?" she asked Ozzie.

"Phel's a fairy creature, he's *made* of magic."

"How can that be?" Emily's rational mind wondered. "We can touch him! We can see him!" She shook her head. "I don't know what to believe, anymore."

"Prove it," Adriane said to Phel. "Show us magic."

The corners of Phel's thin mouth turned up into a smile. Tiny pinpoints of light sparkled across his fur. Then as if by some silent signal, dozens of animals began to emerge from the forest. Emily rubbed her eyes. "I think I'm seeing things," she whispered.

"Emily, that's ... that's a ... " Adriane stammered incredulously. "What is that?"

Before them stood a pony with resplendent wings of bright orange and yellow, like those of a butterfly. A dozen Jeeran stepped forward, followed by a host of other creatures. Some had wings, some had scales, one had the body of a cat and the head of a bird. Emily could not even begin to identify the others.

Then she caught her breath. A magnificent white owl with glowing turquoise eyes hobbled to a halt at her feet. Her heart, so full of wonder a moment ago, emptied with a dull ache. The owl's wings glowed a sickly green—just like the burns on the cat.

"My wings can't fly." Emily heard the words in her head as clearly as if they'd been spoken aloud.

"Emily!" Adriane was pointing to the animals.

Emily was taken aback by the tears that ran down Adriane's cheeks. She looked more closely at the other animals. "Oh, no!" she gasped.

"Oh, my." Even Ozzie seemed shocked.

The hind legs and back of one of the jeerans was a patchwork of raw abrasions, all colored with the faint green glow. It swayed slightly, as if just standing up was an effort. The winged pony's flank was slashed by a lightning strike-shaped burn. Some of the animals couldn't walk very well, and others were helping the wounded move along. The duck-like creature she'd met earlier was herding forward several others of its kind, all covered in the noxious glow.

Pain throbbed like a hot coals as Emily felt the animals' misery—but she also sensed a spark of hope that flared in them upon seeing Phel. She gripped Adriane's hand.

A jeeran, its leg crisscrossed with greenish burns, approached Phelonius. Emily held her breath as the purple giant reached out toward the jeeran. Immense but gentle paws touched the animal's sides and legs. The jeeran shivered. Phel's fur shimmered. The brighter he shone, the fainter the green glow became. Then Phel's light faded and the horrible burns were gone!

"How did you do that?" Emily asked, astonished.

He removed his paws and released a cloud of rainbow sparkles that twinkled through the air. The jeeran bent a front leg in a bow to Phel, then danced away, its hooves kicking up dirt and grass.

Adriane turned to Emily, her face full of wonder as one

by one the injured animals approached Phel. As he worked, more and more rainbow sparkles floated and danced over the glade. The air glittered. Rainbow puff flowers sprouted and blossomed. Emily's pain washed away like that of the healed animals, leaving in its place an incredible sense of hope and dreams ... and magic.

Adriane had found Stormbringer herding animals forward and she ran to her friend. "How can this be happening?"

"Magic finds a way, warrior."

Emily looked down at the owl sitting near her. As gently as possible, she lifted it in her arms. Then she turned to Phel.

"I want to help," she said.

9

EMILY HELD THE owl as Phel's great paws stroked its wings. The jewel on her wrist pulsed with a bright blue light. She was concentrating so hard, she was barely aware of Adriane, Ozzie, Stormbringer, and the other animals watching. As the light from her stone mixed with Phel's warm glow, she could *feel* the poison leaving the owl's body; could *sense* its strength returning. Her heart leaped into flight. The owl opened its bright eyes and looked adoringly at Emily. She gently scratched its head and was thrilled to see a glimmer of turquoise and gold run through its feathers.

"There, is that better?" she asked.

"A mouse would be good."

"That was amazing, Emily," Adriane breathed.

Emily laughed as she brushed the soft feathers with her hand. Then she lowered the owl to the ground.

"Ariel likes you." The duck-thing was standing there watching.

"Thank you … I think. Her name is Ariel?"

"Yes."

"What's your name?" Emily asked.

"Ronif," it told her. "I'm a quiffle."

Emily blinked. "My name is Emily. These are my friends, Adriane, Ozzie, and Stormbringer." She pointed to each in turn.

The quiffle looked them over. "Mages!" He waddled away to tell the others.

"Come on, let's help them." Emily got up to carry one of the wounded quiffles to Phel. Adriane joined her.

The sun dropped low behind the trees, its golden rays cutting across the glade, but Emily hardly noticed, too busy holding and soothing the sick and wounded animals while Phel healed them. Adriane and Storm moved among the larger animals, helping them get to Phel.

At last no more animals came forward. Emily sat down, exhausted and exhilarated at the same time. She held the beautiful owl in her lap and gazed at the extraordinary collection of creatures gathered in the glade. They were all watching her. She sensed their joy at being healed, and yet they seemed nervous, darting glances into the woods and up toward the sky.

Adriane approached, half a dozen baby quiffles riding in her pockets, and three more in her arms. Adriane plopped three into Emily's lap, then sat down carefully, so as not to disturb her passengers. Ariel let the tiny quiffles snuggle into her feathers; they cooed happily, and Emily laughed.

"Fantastic!" Ozzie said as he walked over.

"We didn't really do anything," Emily said. "Phel healed them all."

"Don't be so modest."

"Did you see your stone glowing?" Adriane asked. "Like mine did, when I made those trees move."

Emily checked her jewel. It wasn't glowing now.

"Maybe the stones react to magic," she suggested.

"Very possible," Ozzie said. "Phel's flowers are seeding the whole place with magic, the stones could be absorbing it."

"Yeah, maybe they store the magic—like batteries—and let us use it," Adriane ventured.

"Could anyone use these, or … just us?" Emily wondered.

Adriane looked at Ozzie, eyes narrowed. "What else do you know that you haven't told us?"

"Those burns." Ozzie said looking over at the animals. "It's the Black Fire.

I had no idea it was this bad. And they're the ones that made it here. Who knows what's happened to the others left behind."

"No wonder they're all scared," Emily said. "Talk to them, Ozzie."

"Who, me?"

"Tell them everything's going to be all right," Emily added.

"Come on, Ali—Ozzie," Adriane said.

"Oh, all right." Ozzie got up and walked over to the animals. "Hello, I'm Ozymandius, er, Ozzie." The animals all perked up, eyes wide-open, ears pricked forward. The ferret steeled himself and faced the crowd. "I'm an elf."

"You don't look like an elf," Ronif the quiffle remarked.

"That's right, genius! I know I don't *look* like an elf!"

"Go on, Ozzie, you're doing great," Emily said encouragingly.

"I'm from Aldenmor, like you. I grew up in the village of Farthingdale, near the Moorgroves."

Sounds of recognition were heard from the animals.

"It's a secluded Elven place. Too secluded for me—I wanted to explore the world. If I had known any better I would've stayed home!" He surveyed the expectant faces and continued. "One day, I wandered out among the Moorgroves and got lost in the dark forests. Phel found me and brought me to the Fairy Glen, and I actually *met* Fairimentals!"

Murmurs of wonderment surged through the crowd.

Encouraged, Ozzie grew more animated, waving his paws and shuffling back and forth. "They knew I was coming, don't ask me how—who knows the ways of fairies? They told me Aldenmor was in great danger, that soon there would be no place safe."

An animal bugled agreement; Emily thought it was one of the jeerans.

"The Fairimentals are searching for an enchanted place, the source of all magic. They said they needed 'humans' to help. I was to find three mages. A healer—" He paused and looked directly at Emily. "A warrior—" He looked at Adriane. "And a blazing star."

Eyes wide, Emily glanced at Adriane. "Blazing star?" she whispered, perplexed. Adriane shrugged.

Ozzie continued. "I didn't have the faintest idea what they meant, but it's not every day a Fairimental asks for your help. So I followed their directions and somehow ended up getting tossed through some portal and into this world— stuck in the body of a ferret! I don't really know much else. It's kind of fuzzy," he said apologetically. "My giant-sized brain's been compressed to the size of a peanut!"

Ronif stepped forward. "The Fairimentals were right. The Black Fire is destroying our world, poisoning us. If we hadn't found our way here, and if you and the great fairy creature hadn't helped us, we would have died."

"What is Black Fire?" Emily asked.

Ronif turned to her. "It rains from the sky and seeps through the ground, burning all that it touches."

Emily turned to Adriane. "My mom was right," she said. "It's some kind of toxin, or radiation, maybe."

"Now we are refugees here in this strange land," a winged pony said.

"Some of us have left families behind." The speaker was one of the quiffles. The others voiced their agreement. The baby quiffles buried their heads in Emily's arms and started to cry.

Another winged horse stepped forward. "We pegasi know of legends." It looked directly at the two girls. "Old legends say that once, long ago, animals and humans worked together to make magic."

Emily looked down at her stone. *Mage ... healer ... magic ...* The words ran round and round in her head.

Ozzie spoke up again. "If the legends say that animals and humans once worked together, then that's what we are going to do again." He pointed to Emily and Adriane. "The important thing now is that you have friends here. Somehow, we'll figure it all out together."

The animals signaled their approval with bleats and neighs, barks and hisses, quacks and hoots.

"Go, Ozzie!" Adriane cheered.

The sniffling quiffles stared up at Ozzie.

"Hey now, I may be a weasel, but I can still dance!" Ozzie shuffled an elf dance in front of the quiffles. "Look, the wigjig!"

He leaped into the air, twisted, and landed with his arms

outstretched—and fell over backward. The quiffles giggled.

"What I wouldn't give for feet," Ozzie mumbled into the dirt.

Suddenly the ground beside him swirled and he jumped back. The animals looked at one another. Emily and Adriane stared as four small pools of dirt and twigs rose from the ground, spinning into tiny whirlpools.

"Fairimentals ... " someone in the crowd said reverently. Everyone fell silent as the whirlpools danced toward the girls.

Emily and Adriane stood quickly as the whirlpools buzzed around their legs.

"Sankk uuuu ... " The voice seemed to come from the closest whirlpool, and Emily turned to follow it.

"Frrrrienndss ... " came the voice of another.

"Sssssssssrrrrrr ... " another said in a swirling frenzy. It flew apart, twigs and leaves flying.

The first whirlpool spun by even faster. *"Serrrrrrrrrrecch ... "*

"Search. Search for what?" asked Emily, listening hard.

"Hommmmm ... "

"Hommmmmm ... "

"Hommmmm ... " the third cyclone added its tiny voice in a harmonic chorus as the three spun together, weaving in and out and around the girls.

"Please, can't you tell us more?" Emily had bent over to make sure they could hear her.

One tiny tornado spun wildly by her. *"Weecannnotttsttaaayherrrr ... "*

"Er ... I don't mean to be rude, but before you go, you think you could, mmm, like, change me back?" Ozzie whispered.

"*Uucannnnottgoobackk ... *"

The whirlpools were wavering, starting to fall apart, as if the strength it took to communicate was too much for them.

"Please, don't go! Where is home?" Emily was close to tears.

The whirlpools spun faster, trying to hold together for one last message. But with a whisper they blew apart and became the wind.

"Nooo!" Emily cried.

"Emily ... " Adriane said in a hushed tone.

There on the ground before them, a word was etched in the dirt: Avalon.

"Thanks a lot!" Ozzie was jumping up and down.

Avalon.

Emily stared at the word as a cool breeze blew it to dust. What did it mean?

The animals moved about restlessly. Somehow they understood what the Fairimentals were saying: that there was no going back. They were refugees without a home. An unspoken sadness spread through the glade.

"What about the monster?" a little quiffle asked in a tiny voice. A perceptible chill swept through the crowd.

"The dark creature will hunt us down," said a blue rabbit-like animal.

"It's out there somewhere, waiting," a pegasus said ominously.

Phel stepped forward and the crowd parted to let him through. Pinpoints of light sparkled from his shimmering purple fur and a shower of stars gently cascaded over the glade. A sense of calm spread through the animals.

Emily rose and went to Phel. She put her arms around him as far as she could reach and held him close. He made a soft noise. Adriane joined Emily. The little quiffles giggled, and the girls laughed. Slowly others crept up to snuggle in. Emily and Adriane were soon buried in warm animals.

"You, too, Alice." Adriane reached out and pulled Ozzie in.

"Gah!"

For that moment, surrounded by the giant arms and warm magic of Phel, no one was afraid.

STARS WINKED IN a velvet sky as Adriane walked Emily down the road out of the preserve.

"Well, we found the animals," Adriane said at last.

"We sure did." Emily agreed.

"So, what's your analysis of the situation, Doc?" Adriane asked lightly. But she looked tense.

"Well, most of what we know is still pretty vague." Emily felt better analyzing the facts. "But one thing seems sure: these animals have come from another world, and that world is being poisoned by something terrible."

"Go on."

Emily took a deep breath. "Okay, now some kind of doorway between worlds has opened—a portal as Ozzie calls it—and the hurt animals are making their way here, where it's safe."

"But how safe?" Adriane asked.

"And the Fairimentals want us to find something ... a place," Emily continued.

"Avalon. The home of magic."

"Adriane, Ozzie said the Fairimentals need three mages ..."

Adriane looked at her, waiting.

"If we *are* two of them … who's the third?"

"I don't know anything about mages," Adriane said with a shrug. "But I do know we *can't* let Ravenswood be destroyed. Those animals have nowhere else to go!"

"You're right. We have to do something."

"We will." Adriane held up her bracelet, and the striped jewel sparkled in the moonlight.

Emily lifted up her own gem. "Together," she said. A spark flashed between the two stones—a connection forged between friends, a bond that would last forever.

Adriane turned and walked back up the road to the preserve. Emily looked out over the parklands at the warm lights of her house.

Avalon. The word drifted through her mind like a soft breeze as she walked home.

10

THE STONEHILL TOWN Hall was a two-story redbrick building right on Main Street, across from a nicely tended park with a playground and lots of benches and trees. Carolyn parked their green Explorer while Emily searched the crowded parking lot for Adriane and Gran. Then she heard the sputtering of an old pickup truck and looked over to see Gran barreling into a parking space. The ancient engine protested, shuddered, and came to rest.

"Hey!" Adriane jumped out to greet Emily.

"Hey," Emily returned. "Mom, this is Adriane's grandmother."

"Please call me Nakoda," Gran said warmly.

Carolyn held out her hand. "I'm Carolyn Fletcher."

Gran smiled. "It is my pleasure. Emily is a special child."

"She'll do." Carolyn smiled back.

The town hall was jammed. Mayor Davies was up on the podium, listening to people argue back and forth about the Ravenswood Preserve. They were convinced some dangerous predator was killing innocent animals.

Why couldn't these people see how important

Ravenswood was? Emily thought. Suddenly her wrist began to itch like crazy. She checked her bracelet. Her stone was pulsing light! Quickly, she pulled down the sleeve of her sweater to cover it. But she had the strangest sensation that someone was watching her. She looked around the room and her eyes met the bright blue eyes of the blond girl whose friends had teased her at Arrowhead Park.

"Who's that?" Emily asked Adriane in a whisper.

Adriane scowled, "Kara Davies, the mayor's daughter."

"You don't like her much," Emily surmised.

"Who wears pink sweaters and perfectly matched pink sandals? She's such a Barbie!" Adriane crossed her arms over her chest and glared daggers at Kara—and suddenly the jewel on her bracelet sparked. Startled, Adriane covered her wrist

The blond girl's eyes narrowed.

"We think it was a bear!" one of the men Adriane had confronted on the preserve called out. "Almost had it, too."

"And?" the mayor prompted.

"It got away," the hunter scowled. "But we'll get it!"

Emily stiffened. "They're talking about Phel," she whispered to Adriane. But she couldn't dare tell anyone about Phel, that he was magic! How could she explain that he'd *healed* the animals?

The crowd was buzzing. "Place should be closed ... Wild animals near our town—it's too dangerous!" People were clearly upset.

Mrs. Beasley Windor, a very vocal member of the town council stood up. "Let's just cut to the chase here." Her tight black hair, beady eyes, and sharp nose made her look like a hawk. "We can't have dangerous animals running around like a jungle. Ravenswood has a history, but I say it *is* history!"

"The animals need a place to live also!" Emily said more loudly than she'd intended.

"Yeah, they have rights, too!" Adriane echoed.

"Excuse me! Since when do *children* have a voice in town matters?" Mrs. Windor said condescendingly. "Especially those involving public safety!"

"Mrs. Windor, please," the mayor said. "We still need proof of these accusations."

"Oh, really." She walked forward and slapped a letter onto the lectern in front of the mayor. "Why don't you read this, Mayor?" She gave Carolyn and the girls a snide look. "It's a copy of a letter sent to Dr. Carolyn Fletcher from the University of Pennsylvania."

"Uh-oh, this is bad," Adriane said to Emily.

Carolyn glanced at Emily. Emily tried to smile but felt her lips lock into a grimace.

The mayor quickly read the letter. "Well, this settles it then. Health officials from the Centers for Disease Control will be here in two days, so if we can't find a solution to this problem, they will give us one."

"You got that right." Mrs. Windor was smiling. "The place should be shut down and the land properly developed!" she repeated to a chorus of agreements.

"Okay, folks, let's take a break and cool down," the mayor said. "Mrs. Charday, may I speak to you for a minute? You, too, Dr. Fletcher."

Carolyn and Gran rose. Adriane and Emily started to follow, but Carolyn stopped them. "You two wait outside. You think you can do that without creating a town incident?"

Emily knew better than to argue with her mother when she used that tone.

Mortified, the girls left the building and walked over to the park. Except for their moods, the summer night was perfect—low humidity, a cool breeze, and a golden waxing moon.

Adriane kicked at a small rock. "Now what?"

"My mom's gonna kill me about that letter!" Emily wailed. "I wish we had done something else!"

"Shhh, wait, someone's coming," Adriane hissed.

In the orangey glow of a street lamp, Emily saw pink sandals. She and Adriane stared as Kara Davies strolled up to them.

"What?" the blond girl asked. "Is there gum in my teeth?"

"What do you want?" Adriane asked rudely.

Kara didn't seem fazed. "It's a free country. I can walk here if I want to." She looked at Emily. "Almost didn't recognize you without a pile of dogs."

Emily reddened. "I'm Emily Fletcher."

"I'm Kara Davies—"

"We know who you are," Adriane interrupted.

"So, I know who you are, too," Kara replied, not missing a beat.

"Great, now what do you want?" Adriane shot back.

"Nothing … I just thought you could tell me what store in the mall carries those bracelets."

"You can't buy them," Adriane told her with obvious satisfaction.

"I can *buy* anything I want." Kara dismissed Adriane with a flick of her hand.

"Well, you can't *buy* these!" Adriane held up her arm and shook the bracelet in front of Kara's face. The stone blazed to life with a fierce golden fire. Startled, Adriane quickly pulled her wrist behind her back.

Kara's bright blue eyes were as wide as saucers. "Wow! How'd you make it glow like that? Batteries?" she guessed.

Adriane looked at Emily. Neither girl replied.

Kara tried a new ploy. "Maybe I can help you and your wild animals, if you give me one of your bracelets," she offered slyly.

"No way!" said Adriane.

"Wait a minute," Emily said. "Maybe Kara *can* help us. If we show her where we got these, maybe she could convince her father to help … *all* the animals." She looked meaningfully at Adriane.

"Daddy always listens to me," Kara boasted. "But first you have to take me to the store where you got those."

"Read my lips," Adriane stated. "No *way!*"

"Adriane, maybe Kara can find her own stone," Emily suggested.

"Sure, I'm a power shopper," Kara smiled, showing perfect teeth. "And you can just tell me where in the mall, you wouldn't even have to go with me."

"Oh, of course, it would be just horrible being seen with us," Adriane said.

"I just meant it might be easier," Kara replied, as if she were speaking to a three-year-old. She twirled the ends of her long blonde hair.

Emily nudged Adriane.

"Okay," Adriane agreed. "But we have to take you there."

"And you have to promise that whatever we show you, you'll keep secret," Emily added.

"Of course," Kara dropped her voice to a whisper. "I understand how important it is to keep cool about fashion. Pretty soon everyone would have one."

"Geez! That's not the point!" Adriane burst out.

Kara gave a well practiced 'Like what's with her?' look.

"So, you promise?" Emily prompted.

Kara was getting impatient. "Yes, yes, fine."

"Emily!" Emily looked up to see her mother calling her from the steps of the town hall. Gran stood beside her. Others were leaving the building. Evidently the meeting was over.

"Coming!" Emily called back. She turned to Kara. "Tomorrow at noon, meet us out by the baseball diamond in the playing fields and we'll take you into the woods."

"You found those in the woods? How disgusting! Forget it!"

Adriane shrugged. "Okay, fine, we'll do it without you."

"Wait, lemme see those again." Kara grabbed for Emily's wrist.

Brilliant turquoise light flared from the blue-green gem. Kara jumped back. It was so fast it might have been a trick of the light. This time it was Emily who was shocked by the vivid flare of her jewel.

Kara stared with her mouth open. "Okay, noon," she said.

AS THEY DROVE home, Carolyn filled Emily in her conversation with Gran and the Mayor. Too many people were worried about dangerous predators; and even the mayor had to admit an interest in the money a new development would bring the community.

"The university analysis presents more immediate

problems," Carolyn went on.

Emily sank into her seat. "I shouldn't have hidden it. That was pretty dumb, huh?"

"Yes, it was. Especially since the mayor's office faxed me a copy only a few hours later." She glanced at Emily. "Since you read it, you know they detected an unidentified toxin and they recommended quarantine."

"But they can't do that!"

"Health officials will be here in a few days. Unless we can show them the place is safe, it may have to be shut down."

Emily softly rubbed the jewel under her sweatshirt sleeve. She and Adriane *had* to figure out how to help Phelonius and the animals. Time was running out.

11

IT WAS A quarter to noon when Emily left her house. With the Pet Palace population slowly dwindling as vacations ended, her chores were taking less time. She thought hard as she crossed the picnic grounds and headed over to the baseball fields. The townspeople were wrong—Phel was no monster! But they were also more right than they knew—something evil was in those woods and it was stalking all kinds of animals. How could they fight *that*? How—

"How is this supposed to work?"

Emily looked up to find Kara standing on home plate. The blond girl wore a silver silk jacket over a pink T-shirt that said ROCK STAR in fake silver gems. Light green shorts and strappy sandals completed the outfit.

"Oh, hi." Emily said. In her concern for the animals, she had almost forgotten about Kara.

"What are we supposed to do?" Kara demanded. "Just wander around in the woods? It's creepy—and dangerous. Do we have a treasure map or something?" Her steely gaze bore into Emily.

"How 'bout we just saddle up and follow the old Injun

trail?" Adriane had come up from the other direction.

"Do you *always* wear black?" Kara remarked, taking in Adriane's black jeans, black T-shirt, and black hiking boots with clear disdain.

"Just until they invent a darker color," Adriane retorted. She tossed her long black hair over her shoulder. "Let's go."

"Where are we going, exactly?" Kara asked.

"You're about to get the grand tour of the Ravenswood Wildlife Preserve," Adriane told her. "We show you around and then take you home. That's it." She turned and walked back up toward the road. "And no lectures."

"Hey!" Kara ran to catch up. "What about those stones?"

"If you find one, we'll throw you a party," Adriane said.

"What's with her?" Kara asked Emily.

"She's worried about the animals that live in the preserve," Emily told her. "And if the place is closed down, she and Gran will have to move."

"Why don't you and *Gran* just move into a normal house?" Kara pressed.

Adriane stopped and faced Kara. "Look, just stay behind us and try not to say anything too stupid, *please!*"

"You know, you should really try a little bran in your diet."

"Someone shoot me now!" Adriane strode quickly up the path.

Emily and Kara hurried to keep up with Adriane as she forged into the woods. The sun poured golden beams through the overhead branches and cool breezes blew the leaves, creating shifting patterns of light and shadow across the forest floor.

Kara had only one thing on her mind. "So, what do I

look for? Minerals? Quartz crystals? I have a book on gems in my backpack." She slung off her leather pack and began digging in it.

"You do? That's really cool." Emily was impressed. Adriane moved on ahead, not wanting any part of the conversation.

"Here, look." Kara pulled out a small, fat book. "See? *Identifying Minerals and Gems.* It's grouped by structure, composition, and luster. The structure is the shape, composition is the purity of the stone, and luster is color."

"Wow." It struck Emily that Kara might not be as shallow as she seemed. She might even be pretty smart.

Kara continued. "Here's the really precious stones, emeralds, sapphires—and my favorite—diamonds!" Kara said. "We can look up your stone in here, too."

Emily held up her wrist as Kara flipped through the pages, trying to find a match. "We made our own bands," she commented self-consciously. "It was Adriane's idea."

Kara barely glanced up. "Not bad. I have some silver chains that'll look much better. I'll get you one."

"I love silver, thanks," Emily said.

"Here, looks like aventurine." Kara pointed to the page. "Properties include protection and healing."

Emily's hazel eyes widened. What a coincidence that she, of all people, should pick up a healing stone! Sunlight reflected off the stone, sending shimmers of color through it.

Kara was mesmerized. She softly touched the gemstone. Blinding shafts of blue and green light flared from the stone.

Both girls screamed and Emily jerked her hand back.

Adriane wheeled around and ran back. "What happened?"

"I don't know, my stone, it just—" Emily began.

"That was so awesome!" Kara exclaimed. "I've never seen anything like that!"

"What did you do?" Adriane asked Kara accusingly.

"Easy, Godzilla, I didn't do anything. Her stone just lit up like a sparkler."

Adriane glared. Kara beamed.

Adriane turned to Emily. "Are you okay?"

"I'm fine." Emily answered. The gem, in its woven bracelet, was now back to normal. "That was so weird."

"I have the perfect silver chain for *my* jewel," Kara went on excitedly.

Adriane ignored her. "We're coming up to the topiary gardens. Over there." She pointed to a garden of living sculptures. There was a lion, a giraffe, an elephant, even a dinosaur all carefully carved out of magnificent foliage. "The topiary gardens are of the most amazing gardens on the estate."

"Oooh, look!" Kara bent over and picked up a sparkly stone. She studied it, scrunched her nose, then tossed it away. "What'd you say?"

"Never mind."

As they walked into the garden, even Kara seemed impressed with the carefully sculptured hedges. "Wow, tree animals! Cool!"

Adriane continued. "First designed in 1920, each of the hedge sculptures is supposed to represent an animal that was on the preserve at that time."

"I thought we were in a 'no lectures' zone," Kara commented.

"Oh, yeah." Adriane and Kara actually smiled at each other.

"And another thing," Kara continued, "these hedge sculptures can't possibly represent the animals that were on the preserve."

"What do you mean?" Adriane asked.

"Hellloo! That's a unicorn, and that's ... like, a dinosaur! I'm pretty sure the hedge-a-saurus has been extinct for like a billion years."

"Maybe they represent animals that were just visiting," Emily said.

"Ooookay." Kara skipped ahead through the tall hedges. Out of the topiary gardens, the lawn sloped downward. Kara stopped as Ravenswood Manor loomed ahead like a gigantic haunted house nestled in the woods. "Are you related to the Addams Family?" Kara quipped.

"Very funny," Adriane replied. "You've never seen Ravenswood Manor?"

"Just in some old pictures."

"They used to have tours here," Emily said.

"Big business on Halloween, I bet," Kara remarked.

Adriane just rolled her eyes. "Come on, we'll go out past the manor. I'll show you the gardens out back."

"What about my stone?"

"We said you *might* find one," Adriane said.

Kara crossed her arms and pouted.

"We *could* look around a bit more," Emily suggested.

"All right!" Adriane led them to the side of the manor and onto another path. They were soon in deep woods and the air was cool and damp. Above, the boughs seemed woven together into a solid canopy of green.

Something rustled in the trees.

"What was that?" Kara whispered nervously.

113

"Just animals," Emily reassured her. "They won't hurt you."

"This is creepy. It's like they're following us."

"They probably never saw anything like *you* before," Adriane said sarcastically.

"On any other day, I might take that as a compliment." Kara studied the ground around her. She gingerly picked up rocks and pebbles, compared them to pictures in her book, and placed some neatly in her backpack.

"Remind me again why she's here," Adriane grumbled to Emily.

"To convince her father to keep the preserve safe."

"Ugh, bugs!" Kara announced behind them. "And I bet there's poison ivy all over here."

"Just keep looking for stones," Adriane shot back over her shoulder. "They could be anywhere."

She leaned in toward Emily again. "And what about the CDC?" she continued. "How are we gonna get through that inspection?"

"I don't know," Emily admitted.

"I don't think they have a listing for 'Black Fire.'"

Over the next hour, Kara amassed a small collection of stones. But none of them glowed, no matter what she did. After a while, she sat down, picked out the nicest stone, and held it tightly in one hand.

Emily noticed and nudged Adriane. The two girls watched, trying not to laugh, as Kara bent over the stone, wrinkle-browed and frowning, a look of intense concentration on her face. Realizing she was being observed, she glared icily at the other girls.

"What are you doing?" Adriane asked incredulously.

"Resting—what's it to you?" Kara got up and tossed the stone away in disgust.

"One of the stones you find is bound to be special," Emily consoled her.

Kara upended her backpack, pouring the stones on the ground. "None of these are any good!"

"Face it, Barbie," Adriane said, "the magic doesn't like you."

Kara jumped to her feet, slinging her empty pack over her shoulder. "That's it! Look, I am Kara Davies, and you are a couple of weirdos. If you think for a minute I'm going any farther into these woods in my brand-new sandals, you're as crazy as you look! I am turning around right now and going to the mall, where normal people go!" She stalked off angrily.

"Now what?" Emily asked. "We can't let her wander around the woods alone."

"She'll be completely lost in about, oh, fifteen seconds," Adriane said.

"Aaahhh!" Kara's scream cut through the forest.

"Correction: ten," Adriane said. "Come on."

Emily and Adriane cut back in the direction of Kara's voice. They found her off the main trail, on a smaller path, looking down into a ravine.

"What now? Did you see a bee?" Adriane taunted.

Kara pointed to a gully ahead of her. "What's that?"

Emily looked—and her breath caught in her throat. With a cry, she slid down the incline.

"Emily, wait!" Adriane cried. But all of Emily's senses were focused on the wounded creature that lay there, half buried under debris. Carefully, she cleared away the branches and wet leaves. As if in a dream, she saw her stone pulsing wildly with blue light. She felt light-headed.

"Ariel!" she cried.

The owl lay in the gully, her body torn and bruised almost beyond recognition. One wing was mangled and bent at an impossible angle. A sickly green glowed in spots on the owl's body. Carefully, Emily felt the owl's chest to see if she was breathing. She was alive—just barely.

"Ugh! That's disgusting!" Kara said, peering down.

"I need something to carry her in!" Emily called up.

"Leave it, it's dead," Kara said. "Aahh—hey!"

Adriane was pulling Kara's silk jacket off her shoulders.

"What are you doing? That's a DK!" Kara protested.

Throwing it down to Emily, Adriane said, "If either of us had a jacket, believe me, we wouldn't want yours."

Emily gently wrapped the owl in Kara's jacket, then carefully carried her up out of the ravine.

"Is she all right?" Adriane asked.

"No. We have to get her to Phel—quickly."

"What about *her*?" Adriane nodded in Kara's direction.

Kara stood, silently fuming.

Emily's only concern was the owl. "Ariel's going to die if we don't get her to Phel right now!"

"Let's go. This way." Ignoring Kara, Adriane started down the small path. Emily followed, cradling Ariel in her arms. When Kara realized she was being left behind, she ran to catch up.

"Where are you going?" she demanded.

Adriane whirled around. "We need to get this animal to where she can be healed!"

"She's hurt bad," Emily said softly.

"Well, lucky I found her, huh?" Kara said. Then she

paused. "What's a Phel?"

"Look, just remember your promise," Adriane said sharply. "You tell no one about what we show you."

"I knew it! A secret place you weren't telling me about!" Kara's eyes sparkled.

"I'm serious! Promise!" Adriane insisted.

"Okay, okay, I promise," Kara said.

Emily hurried along the trail, Adriane at her side. Kara was falling behind, her sandals no match for the logs and rocks that littered the forest floor.

They entered the archway of trees and rounded the Rocking Stone as a voice called out, "There you are! Did you bring any food? Oh no, what's happened?"

Kara caught up a moment later, looking up at the immense boulder. She stepped past it into the glade and her eyes opened wide. "Wow!" She looked from the lovely willow trees to the clear crystal waters of the pond. Flowers bloomed everywhere and rainbow sparkles drifted lightly in the air.

"Ozzie, where's Phel?" Emily was frantic.

"Probably out spreading magic seeds," Ozzie replied.

Out of the corner of her eye, Emily could see Kara approaching. Clearly, the blond girl intended to meet whomever Emily was talking to. "Hello, I'm—" Kara began. Then she stopped, puzzled, and looked around.

"Who's that?" Ozzie asked.

Kara peered at the brown-and-gold ferret, then back at Emily. "Who said that?" she asked. When no one answered, she shook her head, confused. "What is this place?"

"Just another garden," Adriane said.

"Oh really! Well, I've never seen flowers like these!"

"Phel, where are you? Phel?" Emily was beginning to panic as she paced around the glade, cradling the owl.

"Phel, phel, phel..." Kara looked about. "What is a Phel, and where can I find a jewel—hey!" Ozzie was standing in front of her. "Get away, you ... rat!"

Ozzie rose on his rear legs and crossed his arms. "Who you calling a rat?"

"Aaahhh, it's talking!" she shrieked.

Kara started to back away. She turned to her left and saw a winged horse! A green-striped deer watched her. Everywhere she looked, another bizarre animal appeared. Kara whirled around—and came face to face with a huge purple creature. Two gigantic eyes stared at her

"A purple bear!" she shrieked, backing away.

"He is not a bear," Adriane said calmly.

In spite of her fear for Ariel, Emily couldn't help noticing the interest the animals were showing in Kara.

"Who are ... what are all these ... these ... *things*?" Kara stammered.

Phel reached forward with huge paws.

Kara grabbed Adriane. "Stay away from me, you bear!"

"Let go of me! He won't hurt you!" Adriane said.

Panicked, Kara looked up at the giant creature. Phel spread his arms wide. The air seemed to swirl—and something formed between his huge paws. It looked like a circle in the air. Phel spread his paws apart, and the circle widened, revealing ... *stars*. Pinpoints of light were strung out along what looked like a web—almost like a giant, three-dimensional dreamcatcher.

"It's a fairy map!"

Kara's head jerked around. The ferret jumped up and

down next to Phel. More animals were gathering around, watching.

Phel suddenly released the web of stars and it floated over Kara, gently cascading down like a starry rain. She was covered with sparkling dots of light as the web encircled her.

Kara screamed at the top of her lungs, swinging her backpack to bat away the strands of stars. She jumped as if covered in ants, waving her arms and kicking her legs. The magical image tore apart in swirls and vanished.

"Kara, are you all right?" Emily called out.

"The map! It's all gone!" Ozzie sat on the grass, moaning, his head in his paws.

Kara slung her backpack over her shoulder. "I'm getting out of here right now! Keep your dumb stones. I can buy better ones at the mall!" She turned and stormed out past the Rocking Stone.

Adriane turned to Emily. "So much for her helping us."

"Get me out of here!" Kara screamed from behind the rock. "I'm freaking out!"

"Adriane, you'd better take her back," Emily said nervously. "I'll help Phel with Ariel."

Adriane grimaced. "I'll be back as soon as I can." She headed out. "Keep your shorts on," she yelled to Kara.

"You didn't tell me you had bears here—and whatever else you're hiding!" Kara shouted.

As their voices faded into the distance, Emily walked over to Phel. He was sitting by one of the trees. As she lay the owl before him, she realized he was different now: weaker. His color wasn't as vibrant, he seemed duller, with a tinge of gray … and no rainbow flowers bloomed about his feet.

"Please, you can help, can't you?" she asked, gazing up

at his eyes.

Phelonius looked from the owl to Emily. A tear ran down his cheek. She could feel Phel's pain, a deep sadness, and it hit her—he did not have the magic left to heal the owl.

Emily felt the familiar sting of helplessness well up inside. Suddenly her hands were covered by Phel's large paws. Her stone began to glow softly with pale blue light. Phel moved Emily's hands over the owl.

She recoiled, instantly knowing what Phel wanted from her.

"I can't," said Emily, tears spilling from her eyes. "I'm not a *real* healer. I couldn't even help that poor cat!"

As Phel pulled his paws away, Emily blinked back the tears. Her gem had been transformed! It was now a polished, crystalline blossom glistening with rainbow sparkles. It looked exactly like one of Phel's magic puff flowers.

Emily held her breath. She hardly noticed when Phel guided her hands back to the owl, holding them steady as she touched the snowy feathers.

She gasped.

Her stone pulsed faster, beating along with her heart. Suddenly she felt the owl's heartbeat, out of sync with her own, weaker. Phel closed his eyes and Emily concentrated. She *willed* the owl's heart to beat with hers.

Slowly the wounded owl stirred. Emily felt something pushing against her, a sense of weakness, of pain. But she couldn't break its grip. She felt the owl slipping away. "No! Stay with me!"

The feeling of loss engulfed her, threatening to pull her into a dark abyss of despair. It was overwhelming. She'd lost so much already—her dad, her friends, her home. Then she thought of the cat, how she had failed when she needed her most.

"No!" Emily cried out. She reached deep inside. All her emotions seemed to rise up at once and the jewel erupted with jagged blue light. It swirled around her wrist, spreading up and down to cover her arm and her hand. Concentrating hard, she willed the light to flow over the owl. Focus ... focus on the heartbeat. Pulse ... pulse ... pulse ... steady, strong ... And then she *felt* the owl's heartbeat lock with her own. The jewel and both hearts began to beat as one. Steady, strong ... The light faded ... The owl stirred and opened her eyes.

Emily threw herself into Phel's arms, crying and laughing at the same time.

"I can't believe it. We did it!" she said through her tears.

"I think that counts as magic," Ozzie commented.

12

"YOU SHOULD HAVE seen Ozzie, he was so impressed. He was bragging to all the animals how *he* discovered you, a real healer!" Adriane laughed.

Emily was on the phone in her room, listening to her friend. She had run right home with Ariel. Even if the owl seemed healed, she wasn't taking any chances. Only after her mom gave the owl a clean bill of health did Emily relax.

"I only helped Phel, and it was pretty scary," Emily said, not wanting to talk about *how* scared it made her feel. "How did you do with Kara?"

Adriane snorted. "She blabbered the whole way back about how Ravenswood should be fenced off and locked up tight."

"Well, we had no choice, we had to take her to the glade," Emily said.

"Yeah … " Adriane's voice trailed off..

"What's the matter?" Emily prompted.

"That thing Phel did to Kara—" Adriane started.

"What was it?"

"Ozzie said it was a gift from the Fairimentals, a fairy

123

map."

"A map? Of what?" Emily asked.

"Maybe where the animals came from?"

"Or where they're supposed to go." Emily remembered the word left in the dirt:

Avalon.

"Something is going on here, Emily, and you and I are the only ones who know," Adriane said.

"And Kara," Emily reminded her.

"Yeah." Adriane paused. "We have to do something before Barbie opens her big mouth."

"Like what?"

"I think we should go and try to talk to the mayor ourselves."

"I don't know."

"We can say we're returning her jacket," Adriane suggested.

"I guess we can try," Emily said.

"Good. Meet me tomorrow. Ten sharp at town hall."

THAT NIGHT, EMILY couldn't sleep. She pictured Phel, alone in the woods. Well, not really alone. She had to laugh when she thought about Ozzie, insisting on staying with the big creature to protect him. Poor Ozzie, so far from his home, and the other animals, scared and lost in a strange world. Emily realized she was talking about creatures out of some dream, as if the old legends about the woods were turning real. Had magical animals been here before? Had humans and animals really worked together in the past? What was a fairy map, and why had Phel given it to Kara … and not her? She felt a pang of jealousy. Not the first time someone was jealous of Kara, that was for sure.

Whatever was going on, one thing was certain. Her life had changed forever, and not just because she wasn't in Colorado anymore. Emily stared at the wondrous jewel in her hand. A stone of healing and she had found it ... or had it found her? She clutched it tightly, as if it really could give her some measure of protection from her doubts and fears. What had happened today with Ariel terrified her. A door had been opened that she didn't want to—*couldn't*—enter.

"There is no going back." Wasn't that what one of the Fairimentals had said? Was she ready to go forward? And where would that path lead? Emily sighed. Ozzie had told Adriane that Phel's fairy map was a gift to Kara. She looked at her jewel. Was this *her* gift?

Quietly, she left her room and ran down to the Pet Palace.

The cat was wide-awake, pacing back and forth. She had been moved to the Pet Palace, since she no longer needed constant care and attention. Emily sensed the cat's restlessness.

Emily walked over and sat down next to her. Moonlight drifted through the window, bathing them both in pale silver light. They stared into each other's eyes.

Emily held up her gemstone and ran it over the cat's mottled and sparse patches of fur. She moved it gently over the odd bumps on the animal's shoulders, trying to think healing thoughts. The stone sparkled softly in the moonlight. She visualized the scars vanishing, the mottled tufts turning to lustrous fur; she closed her eyes tight and concentrated. She opened them and—nothing. The cat looked exactly the same. She lifted her head and licked Emily on the nose.

Maybe healing Ariel had drained the crystal, or she needed Phelonius to guide her. "This is crazy! I can't do this!"

The cat stared at her.

"I'm sorry ... I don't know what else to do." Emily broke down and hugged the cat, sobbing into her neck.

The cat pulled away and turned to pick up something from her bed. When she turned back to Emily, she was holding an orange stuffed lion. Emily took Mr. Snuffles from the cat's mouth. She could swear the cat was smiling at her.

"Taking and giving completes our circle. It's time to let go."

Emily stared at the cat. Maybe she had helped her heal after all. There *was* something more she could do for her, she realized. She reached out to pet her one last time. "We each have to find our own path," she said. Then she went to open the door to the outside.

Moonlight danced in the doorway. A cool breeze ruffled Emily's curls.

"Have faith, healer. The magic is with you, now and forever."

Without a backward glance, the cat walked out into the night. Slowly Emily closed the door and hugged Mr. Snuffles.

THE SKY WAS overcast as Emily navigated her bike into the bike rack by the town hall. The parking lot was full. There seemed to be an unusual amount of activity this morning. It seemed like everyone was rushing about.

"Something's up." Adriane was already at the front steps, waiting for her. "Come on."

Together, the girls walked into the building and crossed the lobby to a desk where a stocky woman with big hair sat fielding phone calls.

"We'd like to talk to the mayor, please," Adriane announced.

"I'm afraid that's not possible," the big-haired lady replied.

"Why not?" Adriane asked.

"First of all, he's not here. Second of all, he's not here."

"We can wait."

"Suit yourself," Ms. Big Hair said.

"What's going on around here, anyway?" Emily asked.

"Haven't you heard? They caught the monster of Ravenswood."

Emily's face went ashen.

"What?" Adriane leaned forward.

A fireman shuffled through to drop some papers on the front desk.

"Who caught what?" Adriane pressed.

"It was a bear," the fireman said. "Can you believe it? A big *purple* bear."

"About time," Ms. Big Hair said. "If you ask me, that place should be shut down. Just stand over there if you want to wait—" By the time she looked up, the girls were gone.

KARA SAT SUNNING in a lawn chair in her backyard. She had everything perfectly laid out within arm's reach: a bowl of chips and trail mix, ice-cold lemonade, suntan oils, and her iPod. Rose-tinted shades covered her eyes and headphones covered her ears. She didn't see Emily and Adriane until they were practically standing right over her.

"Hey, you're blocking my sun!" she complained.

"Where is he?" Emily demanded.

Kara pointed to her headphones. "Can't hear you. Come back next century."

"You told them where he was!" Adriane accused. "You promised you wouldn't tell and you did! How could you?"

Kara sat up and removed her headphones. "Take it easy, Pocahontas. It's not hard to find a twenty-story rock. They're getting a court order to bulldoze the whole place anyway. So go find somewhere else to play."

"Ooohhhhh!" Adriane's eyes flashed with rage.

"Kara, you saw what's going on out there," Emily said, trying to be reasonable. "You saw all those animals."

"I don't know what I saw," Kara replied, clearly uneasy. "All I remember is the monster."

"He's not a monster, he's our friend," Emily told her.

"That figures."

"That's it!" Adriane advanced on Kara, her hands balled into fists. Bright gold fire suddenly flared from Adriane's bracelet.

Kara's jaw dropped. "How did you do that?"

Adriane stared at her gemstone. The stone pulsed with light. "I didn't do anything," she said, more to Emily than to Kara.

Emily turned slowly to Kara. "Maybe *you* did something."

Kara tried, but she couldn't hide her astonishment. "Yeah, right," she scoffed.

Emily held up her wrist. Both Kara and Adriane stared at the incredible crystalline flower that flickered with rainbow sparkles in the sunlight.

"Emily, your stone, it's … " Adriane started.

"Amazing!" Kara finished.

"Phel did it." Emily said.

"The purple bear gave you that?" Kara asked, her eyes wide. Emily moved the jewel closer to her. The stone flashed a bright burst of blue. Emily backed away and the stone cooled.

"You're making it do that," Kara said, eyes glued to the startling gem.

"No," Emily said. "You are. In the woods yesterday, Phel tried to give *you* something—a gift,"

"And you ruined it!" Adriane put in.

Kara bit her lip. "And why would it give *me* a gift?"

"I think, for some reason, you are part of this," Emily told her.

"Part ... of ... what?" Kara asked slowly.

Emily looked to Adriane.

"Phelonius is magic, just like these stones," Adriane explained.

Kara shook her head. "That's the most ridiculous thing ... I ev—" She stopped as Stormbringer and Ozzie walked out from behind the rose garden.

"Aaahhhh!" Kara shrieked, knocking over the bowl of chips as she shrank back from the silver wolf. "Keep that thing away from me!"

Storm stood still and looked into Kara's eyes. The girl was mesmerized.

"Do not be afraid."

Startled, Kara looked around. "What? Who said that?"

"The magic is strong with you."

"There's no such thing as magic," Kara said.

"How do you explain *him*?" Adriane pointed to Ozzie.

Kara turned to Ozzie. The ferret was holding the bowl of trail mix in his paws. "These are delicious! Can I have some juice?" he asked her.

"Plenty of toys do that stuff," Kara said uncertainly.

"Come on, Emily, we don't need her." Adriane turned away, pulling Emily with her.

Emily faced Kara and held up her bracelet again. "Kara, Phel gave us his magic and now he needs our help. Are you in or out?" Emily asked.

Kara's eyes sparkled at the jewel. She focused back on Emily and looked over at Adriane, at the wolf and the ferret, all waiting for her. She scrunched her nose as if making an important decision. "They took it to a warehouse at Miller's Point Industrial Park."

14

LIFE IS CHANGE, Emily's father had told her. *Be ready and excited.* Somehow, she was neither. With Ozzie on her lap, she was seated next to Adriane on the Stonehill town bus, headed toward Miller Point Industrial Park. It had been Kara's idea to take the bus. The blond girl was sitting a few rows in front of them, listening to Earl the bus driver drone on about how the mayor should improve the bus lanes. Ozzie's brown nose pressed against the window as he watched the farmlands sweep by.

Emily turned to Adriane. "Do you think this is crazy?"

"Not any crazier than running around the woods with a dangerous predator loose," Adriane answered with a wry smile.

"It's not crazy to help our friend," Ozzie said.

"Why can't the Fairimentals stay with us, Ozzie?" Emily asked.

"Their magic is bound to another world," Ozzie explained. "They can't survive here for long."

"Like Phel." Emily had to face the truth. Phel had limited time here.

"I don't think he was supposed to use so much of his magic to heal those animals," Ozzie said.

"What *is* he supposed to do?" Adriane asked.

"Seed your world with magic."

"Then why did he heal those animals?" Emily asked.

"I think he did it for you, Emily." The ferret was staring at her. "You are the healer." He turned to Adriane. "And you are the warrior."

"We're thirteen-year-old kids!" Adriane reminded him.

"I know, but the Fairimentals came to you," Ozzie replied. "And you've heard Storm. I thought mistwolves were dangerous, but I was wrong. Storm carries memories of her kind that go back centuries. She knows the Fairimentals sent me to find three mages."

Adriane laughed. "Great. If we're two, who's the third?"

Ozzie looked to the front of the bus where a bored Kara sat.

Adriane flushed. "Oh no! Do *not* even go there!"

"She's trying, Adriane," Emily said. "Let's give her a chance."

Adriane looked out the window. "Forget it."

"I could be wrong, of course," Ozzie said. "Being a ferret wasn't part of the plan."

"Maybe they disguised you," Emily suggested.

"An elf in Stonehill—that *would* get people talking," Adriane added.

"But why did they choose me? I wasn't magical as an elf, and I'm not special now," Ozzie said with a hint of defeat. "I just want to go home."

"Ozzie, whatever reason you're here, I'm glad that you are," Emily said.

Adriane looked at Ozzie. "Me, too."

Ozzie smiled a ferret smile.

The bus pulled into the wide parking lot of Miller's Point. The industrial park covered about a square mile of buildings and landscaped parks. Behind the office buildings, on the far side of the park, was a row of warehouses.

"All right, we're here," Kara announced.

"A real Girl Scout," Adriane muttered.

"Where is he, Kara?" Emily asked.

"In one of those warehouses out back, until some UFO team or something comes to get it," Kara told them.

"But which one?"

"I don't know," Kara replied.

"I just hope we got here in time," Adriane said.

"If it wasn't for me, you would still be walking and you would have shown up in about two weeks!" Kara fumed.

"All right, Kara," Emily intervened. "You were right, it *was* a good idea to catch the bus. Let's go."

The girls made their way along a mosaic pathway between the two main office buildings. They emerged on the other side onto an open green lawn with a small man-made lake, its water reflecting the orange and gold of the setting sun. A family of ducks quacked greetings as the girls passed. Ozzie rode in Emily's backpack as they marched down the road toward the semicircle of warehouses.

"How are we going to get back after we find him?" Emily looked around.

"We'll figure something out," Adriane said. She didn't sound too sure, either.

"Well, I have some magic of my own," Kara smirked.

"Oh?" Adriane's eyebrows rose.

"Yeah. It's called a cell phone." Kara held up her little flip phone.

Emily stopped suddenly. "Trouble."

Adriane and Kara stopped and looked where Emily was pointing. Up around the bend was a guard gate, blocking the entrance to the warehouse section of the park. It was manned by security officers.

"Well, I guess this ends our little rescue expedition," Kara stated.

"No way," Adriane said.

A jeep was approaching the gate from one of the warehouses.

"Then we'll just walk through and tell the guards we're here to pick up the purple bear," Kara snickered.

"Good idea." Adriane closed her eyes. Concentrating hard, she formed an image and locked it in her mind. "Stormbringer," she whispered.

Adriane's jewel pulsed with white-gold light.

Kara couldn't hide her amazement.

A cloud of mist appeared and the great silver wolf materialized. Stormbringer walked forward to greet the girls.

"I heard your call, warrior."

"Can you help us get past that gate without being seen?"

The wolf shimmered as if radiating waves of heat. She seemed to expand, and then she was only soft gray-white mist.

Kara's eyes were wide with disbelief.

"Stay close together," the mistwolf's voice said.

"Hey, watch it!" Kara protested as Adriane pushed her up against Emily.

The mist slowly settled around them.

Slowly they made their way up to the main gate. Two guards sat in the gatehouse watching monitors, while a third paced outside.

"My ear itches," Kara complained under the veil of mist.

A small paw reached out and scratched Kara's ear.

"Eeeek!"

"Ssshhh!" Emily repeated urgently.

The jeep drove up and the gate began to swing open.

Adriane tensed. "Ready?"

The jeep drove past and the gate began to close.

"Go!" Adriane gave Kara a push. They shuffled forward, trying to stay together. Emily looked out through the curtain of mist. It was working! The guards didn't even notice them —

Ringggg ... ringggg ...

The pacing guard stopped and pulled his cell phone from its holster. He held it to his ear, then shook it.

Ringggg ... ringggg ...

"What *is* that?" Adriane whispered in a panic.

"Hello?" Kara said into her phone.

"*Ssshhh!* Keep moving!" Emily said.

The guard was looking around, obviously puzzled.

"Oh, hi, Heather!" Kara covered the end of the phone. "It's Heather," she whispered to the girls.

Adriane pushed Kara forward as the gate swung closed behind them. "Go, go, go!"

"Ooo, really? I love pink. How does it look?"

Adriane grabbed the phone from Kara's hand as they turned into an alley between the first two warehouses.

"This call is, like, *so* over!" she said into the phone and hit the OFF button.

"That was, like, *so* rude!" Kara objected.

The mist lifted, and the wolf reappeared.

"Ha! They didn't even see us!" Kara exclaimed. "Very cool."

Adriane turned to Storm. "Can you find Phel?"

The wolf sniffed the air and took off at a trot. The girls and Ozzie followed. They passed several warehouses, and then Stormbringer led them into a dark alley. They were completely in shadows—the sun was almost gone.

Adriane raced up the steps to a door in the side of the building and tried it. "It's locked!" she exclaimed.

A dog barked and a faint light flashed out beyond the end of the alley.

"What do we do now?" Kara said.

"What about that window?" Emily pointed to a small window partway up the side of the warehouse.

"No one can fit in there," Kara said.

"I can," said Ozzie.

"Okay, let's get him up there." Adriane turned to Kara. "Bend over."

"No *way*!"

Emily looked back as a light flashed off the warehouse wall. "Kara, this is no time for arguments."

Kara, muttering angrily, knelt on the ground. Emily climbed up on her back.

"Owww," the blonde girl complained under the additional weight of Adriane, who hoisted herself up on top of Emily. "Why do I have to be on the bottom?"

"If we fall, you won't get hurt," Adriane explained, deftly balancing herself below the window ledge.

"Oh, good idea," Kara agreed. She wriggled to adjust her position, and Adriane wobbled.

"Stay still!" Adriane balanced herself. "Ozzie, get up here!"

The ferret scampered over Kara and Emily and up into Adriane's arms. She hoisted him up and tried to push him onto the windowsill, but it was still too far. She swung her arm back and flung Ozzie up into the air—but the movement of her arm pulled her over. "Whoaaaah!"

Ozzie went flying as she came toppling down onto Emily and Kara.

They looked up. Ozzie was dangling from the window sill by his front paws. They watched as he hoisted himself up and squeezed through the narrow opening of the window.

Emily grinned. "He made it."

There was a crash, followed by a boom.

The girls rushed to the door and waited. They heard the scampering of little feet across the floor, a few bumps, some thuds, and assorted *args* and *doofs*. Then silence.

Emily looked at the other girls. "Ozzie, are you all right?"

"Yes."

"What are you doing?" Adriane asked.

"I can't reach the door release," Ozzie's muffled voice replied.

"Why don't you use your magic charms?" Kara asked sarcastically.

Adriane turned to Emily. "Let's see if we can lift him."

"You think?" Emily looked doubtfully at her bracelet.

"Like when I made those trees move."

Kara raised her eyebrows.

"Okay, what do I do?" Emily asked.

"Concentrate really hard," Adriane said. "Picture Ozzie floating up to the lock."

Emily held her gem close to Adriane's, closed her eyes, and concentrated as hard as she could.

"Ooh!" Ozzie exclaimed from behind the closed door.

"What's happening?" Adriane asked.

"I'm on my tiptoes! Try harder!" Ozzie called back.

Flashlight beams bounced around the entrance to the alley.

"Hurry, the guards are coming!" Kara pushed at their shoulders.

"Stop it, I can't concentrate!" Adriane shot back.

"Anyone there?" a guard called out.

"Oh, hurry it *up!*" Kara pushed harder at the girls.

A flashlight beam swept the alley.

"Would you quit shoving?" Adriane snapped, turning back to Kara.

Kara's hand slipped off Adriane's shoulder and landed on the two jewels. The stones exploded with a flash of light.

"Whoooooaahhhhh!"

Thump!

Crash!

Something inside slammed against the ceiling and came crashing back to the floor. " … Ooooh!" Ozzie's voice sounded wobbly.

"Sorry," Kara said, pulling her hand back.

"A little more subtle," Emily suggested.

Kara lightly touched the stones. They pulsed with bright light as Emily and Adriane concentrated on floating Ozzie up to the doorknob.

"Upseee!" Ozzie was up.

The latch clicked open and the girls tumbled inside. Storm padded in behind them.

"We did it!" Emily exclaimed. Looking around the dark room, she held up her jewel and willed it to shine. She smiled as a pale blue light spilled over the entryway. Adriane added a soft golden glow.

Three darkened hallways ran off in separate directions.

"This is nuts!" Kara shook her head. "We're breaking and entering *and* using illegal magic stuff!"

"Magic is not illegal," Adriane shot back.

"I bet it is, too! How come, like, the President doesn't have this?"

"Sshhh, quiet!" Emily ordered. "Can you two please stop arguing for two minutes! Let's just find Phel and get out of here."

Storm sniffed and headed down the middle hallway. Kara and Adriane moved to follow at the same time and found themselves wedged in the doorway.

"You first, Princess." Adriane bowed to Kara.

"Oh no, after you," Kara said, bowing back.

"No, no, I insist." Adriane swept her arm toward the hall.

"Just come *on!*" Emily barged her way past the others and strode ahead.

The hallway led to what looked like a large storage area. In the dim light, Emily could make out a ramp up to a loading dock on the far side; the large, sliding garage door was shut. So, that's how they got him in here, she thought.

"Phel!" Emily called out in a whisper. "Are you in here?"

Something massive moved in the darkness.

Emily sidestepped, keeping close to the wall.

"Well, is it in here or—" Kara stepped forward, screamed, and disappeared.

"What happened?" Adriane moved in behind Emily.

Emily and Adriane inched forward. In front of them was a huge pit. Their glowing jewels cut swathes of weird light across the wide space. Phel lay on his back on the floor—with Kara standing on his belly.

"Hey, look what I found," she said.

Two gigantic eyes opened, blinked, then stared up at the startled girls.

"Phel! Are you all right?" Emily noticed the steps and was quickly made her way down.

"Did you find himmmaahhhh … " Ozzie bolted into the room, his momentum taking him right over the edge of the drop. He bounced up Phel's belly and looked into a giant eye. "Phel! Thank goodness!"

Phel reached out giant paws and engulfed the ferret.

"Gaaaaooof!" was all Ozzie could say.

Adriane pointed toward the loading dock door. "We can get him out that way!"

Emily gently touched Phelonius. She could sense his weakness. She pushed the fear back. "We have to get you out of here."

Together, the three girls got Phel up and onto his feet. He was frighteningly light for something so enormous. Holding Ozzie under one arm, he shuffled along as they pushed and pulled him up the ramp toward the loading dock.

Adriane started hitting every button she could find to open the big door.

"Doesn't this place, like, have any alarms?" Kara asked.

With a loud *whhirr*, the door started to open. A horn blasted through the night. It rose to a crescendo, then started again. A second horn blared across the compound, followed by a third.

"Does that answer your question?" Adriane said.

"Let's go!" Emily ordered.

They pushed Phel out the door and down the exit ramp. Spotlights flared, flooding the compound.

"What are we going to do?" Kara screamed.

Everywhere they turned, searchlights skimmed the ground, trying to trap them in bright light. Men were yelling and dogs were barking.

"Stay where you are!" a loud voice shouted over a megaphone.

"We are in such major trouble!" Kara wailed.

"Hurry, come on, Phel, we have to run!" Emily pleaded, trying to push him to move faster.

"This is all your fault!" screamed Kara. "You forced me to come here! I'm going to be grounded for, like, five years!"

"You were the one who got him caught in the first place!" Adriane screamed back.

"Stop it! *Stop it!*" Emily shouted. Her gem exploded, sending shafts of blue light shooting into the night. Spotlights burst to pieces and went dark. Sirens blared in the distance.

Stormbringer's frightening growl made the girls turn. The wolf was crouched and poised to attack. Three black guard dogs, barking wildly and baring vicious teeth, were running straight for them.

Adriane raised her stone.

"No!" Emily grabbed Adriane's arm. "We can't hurt them!"

The girls huddled together, shaking, against Phel's side.

"Hey, you! Ever seen a talking ferret?"

The dogs skidded to a halt, turned, and sprang up the loading dock ramp. A small furry creature leaped onto the rope pulley above the ramp, out of range of their snapping teeth.

"Ozzie!" Emily screamed.

Phel blinked great, sad eyes.

Kara shoved herself forward. "Security!" she called. "I'm Kara Dav—mmph!"

Adriane clapped her hand over Kara's mouth. "Are you crazy?" she hissed.

Phel's huge arms came down around the girls.

"To be here with you two? Yes!" Suddenly Kara looked down.

Her feet were no longer on the ground.

Phel was rising up into the air.

Kara screamed.

"Hold on!" Adriane grabbed onto Phel's fur.

"Ozzie!" Emily cried, struggling to break free of Phel's grasp.

The dogs barked and jumped, trying to grab the ferret from the swinging rope.

Storm shimmered into mist and snaked past the dogs. They looked in confusion at the mist.

Ozzie swung the rope over the dogs and jumped. He skidded down the ramp and ran for his life. The dogs barked and bounded after him.

"Wait for me!" Ozzie burst down the alley, inches in front of the snapping jaws of a black Doberman.

Emily slid down Phel's leg. Adriane reached down and grabbed onto Emily's right arm. Emily extended her left arm, reaching down …

"Hurry, Ozzie!" Adriane yelled.

The dogs would have him in seconds.

Emily slid right to the edge of Phel's giant foot.

"Emily!" Kara shrieked.

"I got her." Adriane had hold of Emily's leg.

Emily stretched her arm out, fingers clasping …

"Jump, Ozzie!" she yelled.

Ozzie closed his eyes and leaped. Emily caught his paw and pulled him into her arms. Below, guards and dogs grew smaller and smaller as Phel rose above the industrial park and drifted into the night.

THE SKY WAS ablaze with the orange-golden light of the full moon. Phelonius glided silently on his back, like a great sky whale, high above the countryside.

"Don't you ever do something like that again!" Emily squeezed the ferret in a hug and handed him to Adriane.

"That was the bravest thing I've ever seen." She hugged him, too. "You're okay, Ozzie."

Ozzie opened his arms and reached for Kara.

She scrunched her nose at him. "Nice job, ferret." With a quick glance to make sure Emily and Adriane weren't watching, she kissed Ozzie. "You ever tell anyone I kissed a ferret, I'll have you stuffed!"

Ozzie winked. "Our secret."

The girls and Ozzie sat on Phel's belly, looking out in

total amazement. No one knew what to say. They were flying—being carried through the sky by a creature made of magic! Below, the streetlights and houses of Stonehill looked like exquisite toys.

"Hey!" Kara exclaimed suddenly, leaning over to the side. "I didn't know the Feltners had a pool! And they never invited me over!" She sat back, crossed her arms, and pouted.

Emily and Adriane exchanged glances and started to laugh. After a minute, Kara began to laugh with them. Howls of laughter spilled into the night as they glided peacefully over the treetops, leaving the lights of the town to fade in the distance.

Behind them a dark winged shadow rose above the orange-gold moon. It closed in for the kill.

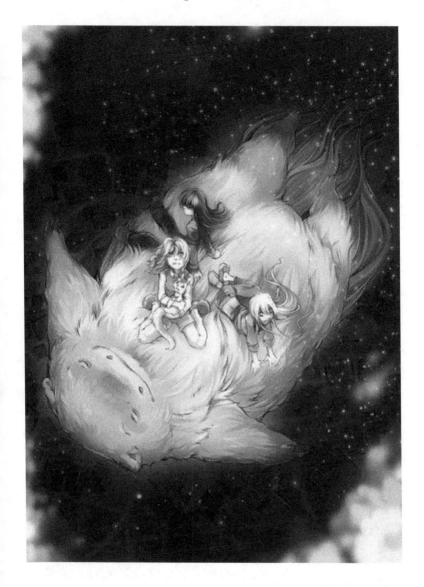

15

PHEL DRIFTED ON a sea of clouds. Kara raised her arms, her long hair furling in the breeze like a golden flag. Adriane searched the dark forests that appeared and disappeared between the low clouds.

Emily was studying Phel. He had been so weak back at the warehouse. How much magic was he using to fly? What would happen if he ran out? Would he come apart like those whirlwinds of dirt and twigs? She peered anxiously over his side.

"We have to get him home," Ozzie told her, seeing the worry on her face.

"How, Ozzie?" she asked.

"We have to find that portal and open it."

"How much longer does he have?"

Ozzie looked down. His silence was answer enough.

Kara was hanging over Phel's side. "Look. An arrow."

"That's not an arrow, that's the Rocking Stone," Adriane scoffed.

Kara shrugged. "Looks like an arrow," she repeated.

Emily narrowed her eyes. Kara was right: from this

height, the ancient stone looked like a skinny finger reaching out … or pointing.

"Aluns," Emily said.

Adriane and Kara looked at her.

"Aluns," she repeated. "It's a Lenni-Lenape word meaning arrow. I found it on the Web. The Rocking Stone is supposed to point to a spirit door, a gateway—"

"Or … a portal," Ozzie said.

All four looked down.

"It looks like it's pointing to that clearing!" Adriane exclaimed.

"The glade?" Emily asked.

"No. Just beyond, to the left."

Out of nowhere, a dark shape swept past, sending Phel careening to the right.

"What was *that*?" Adriane asked nervously.

"I don't want to find out. Hurry, Phel!" Emily called out.

Phel turned towards the Rocking Stone and swooped into dense clouds.

For a moment a shadow was visible against a cloud. Something huge, with gigantic wings.

"Over there." Kara pointed.

Emily and Adriane looked, but it was gone.

They peered around anxiously.

"Hurry, Phel!" Emily called.

The clouds swept past, then parted like a curtain. The monster hung in the sky before them. Phel was on a collision course with two red-hot demon eyes and rows of razor teeth. The monster roared thunder and Black Fire erupted from its mouth to explode against Phel's shoulders. Kara screamed as Phel dropped like a rock, billowing green and black flames.

Wind whipped Emily's hair into her face. "Phel!" Her jewel flared blue and bathed Phel in a blanket of light, extinguishing the flames.

Phel dove low and pulled up in a sweeping arc, careening toward the trees at an alarming speed.

"Left!" Adriane yelled, leaning hard.

"Right!" Kara shrieked, pulling in the opposite direction.

The girls flattened themselves against Phel's body as he swept up and over the forest canopy. Branches and leaves scraped his back.

"We're going to crash!" Kara yelled.

"Adriane!" Emily shouted.

She reached across Kara to clasp Adriane's hand. Sparkles ran across Kara's body and the stones glowed bright. "We need to slow Phel down!"

"I got it," Adriane closed her eyes.

Brilliant rainbow light arced from the gems and spread into a canopy above them. A parachute! Emily gripped Adriane's hand as Phel's descent slowed.

"Hold on!" Adriane yelled.

Kara put her head down and closed her eyes. Emily and Adriane held the rainbow tight. Ozzie wedged himself under the girls.

Phel soared past the Rocking Stone. With a final effort, he skirted the treetops and went down, bouncing hard on the ground. Emily's teeth ground together with the jolt. The rainbow burst apart, leaving a sparkling trail as Phel's body dug a long, shallow furrow in the grass. He came to a stop at the edge of the field.

Emily was sprawled sideways across Phel's chest. Kara was hanging upside down, halfway down his side. Ozzie was stuck under Phel's paw.

Adriane rolled over and hit the ground. "Are you all right?" She helped Emily and Kara slide down. Ozzie jumped off to examine Phel.

"Thank you for flying Air Phel." Kara rubbed her head.

"Help him up," Emily told them.

Together they pushed Phelonius to a sitting position. The back of his head and shoulders was glowing with the evil green poison. It was eating away at him, spreading down his back. Parts of him were becoming transparent.

"Emily, you have to help him!" Ozzie pleaded.

Phel opened his eyes and looked at Emily.

"Tell me what to do!" she begged.

Phel's paw was blinking in and out.

Emily raised her stone and concentrated. The gem flashed blue light as she pushed hard with every ounce of will she had. She felt the dark power of the Black Fire. It was overwhelming, threatening to crush her.

"Help me!" Emily felt her face grow wet from sweat and tears.

Adriane raised her stone. It glowed hot white gold.

"Kara!" Adriane yelled.

Kara stood between them and touched both stones. Golden fire swirled up her arm from Adriane's gem. Kara closed her eyes. Her long blonde hair flared as the magic passed through her, down her other arm, and flowed into Emily's stone. Blue and gold magic collided, and green light flashed from Emily's wrist and streamed out to cover Phel. She felt her heart beating too fast; she was afraid it would explode as she fell into darkness … and then she felt another heartbeat, Adriane's, strong, pure … and Kara's, steady, certain … and Ozzie's, solid, true, pulling her back. Phel began to glow, blue and gold, matching the stones. And the darkness fell away.

The light faded. Phel blinked his eyes. The green poison was gone.

But he was still fading in and out. Emily's throat tightened and she fought back tears. They had stopped the poison, but it was too late. She had failed again, and now she was losing Phelonius.

"What *was* that thing?" Adriane asked.

"A manticore," Ozzie said. "It's bad, real bad."

"What does it want from us?" Kara asked.

"Manticores track magic," Ozzie said.

"Why didn't it get Phel before?" Kara asked

"Maybe Phel's magic was protecting him, hiding him." Ozzie explained

"Phel doesn't have any more magic!" Emily cried.

"But you do," Ozzie said.

The treetops swayed, blown by a sudden wind.

"Hey, what time is it, anyway?" Kara asked in a rush. "I've got a ten o'clock curfew. I gotta go—"

"We need you, Kara," Emily told her.

"You do?" Kara asked.

"We do?" Adriane echoed.

"Every time she's near these stones, they go crazy!"

"What do we do now?" Kara asked.

"We have to send Phel home, back through the portal," Emily said.

"How are we going to do that?" Kara asked.

"Hey! Come back here!" Ozzie yelled.

The girls turned to see Phel slowly lumbering across the field. A few rainbow-puff flowers popped up behind him—

but they withered and collapsed into dust.

The fairy creature's skin was translucent, a ghostly haze in the moonlight. His body seemed to be drifting apart, like Stormbringer turning into mist.

"What's he doing?" asked Adriane.

"Trying to make magic. But he's too weak," Ozzie answered.

"Our stones, concentrate on helping Phel," Emily said.

Emily and Adriane stood next to Kara and held their bracelets in the air. The stones began to glow as Phel raised his arms. An electrical burst of wild magic leaped from the stones, startling the girls. Phel swirled the strands of blue and gold magic in the air. He wove the magic into a circular shape, a web, with a bright silver glow in the center. The shape became a three-dimensional ball that floated in the air in front of him.

Ozzie jumped up and down. "The fairy map!"

The glowing orb grew brighter and brighter. Phel collapsed to the ground growing dimmer and dimmer. The twinkling web floated like a glittering beachball over to the girls. Emily tried to grab it, but it danced away. Adriane jumped for it, but it eluded her grasp. It settled over Kara.

"Take it, Kara!" Adriane said.

"Come on, Kara, take it," Emily pleaded.

Ozzie sniffed the air. Something smelled foul …

Pinpoints of light reflected over Kara's face as she reached out …

A blast of wind tore it from her grasp.

The manticore landed with a ground-shaking *crunch* that rumbled like thunder across the field. Even hunched over, it was massive. It slowly turned its head, and slitted demon eyes bore straight into the girls. Adriane's mouth froze open.

All the color drained from Kara's face. The monster towered over them. The lower part of its body looked like a lion, the upper part resembled a bizarre ape beast with arms muscled like steel cords. Its head was grotesque, with long dripping teeth in a blood-red mouth. Its eyes flared red fire. Gigantic wings unfurled behind its back as it roared. The sound was deafening.

There was nowhere to run.

Embracing the ball of stars, its horrible mouth moved grotesquely as it spoke. "Mine!"

"How could I have been so stupid!" Ozzie cried. "It was after the fairy map."

"If that's what you want, then leave us alone!" Adriane shouted.

"What I want is not your concern, human," it replied, its mouth twisting into a sickening smile. "The fairy creature is dying. It was just a matter of time before it gave up the map."

Emily felt heat at her wrist. The jewel on her bracelet was still pulsing, blazing with light. Adriane felt it too: her stone was also glowing.

The monster stared suspiciously at the gems and growled low in its throat. "My mistress will never allow humans to control magic. Give me those stones!" it roared.

"I would highly recommend you do what it says," Ozzie piped up nervously from behind the girls.

"Fine, let it have them," Emily said. She tried to take off her bracelet but couldn't. "It's stuck!" The more she tried to move it, the more solidly it seemed to cling to her wrist.

"Emily, I can't move mine," Adriane said, panic rising in her voice.

"Me, either!"

"Hurry, give it the stones!" Ozzie was hopping up and down.

The monster reached forward with hands the size of chairs and claws glowing with green poison.

Adriane was desperately pulling and twisting at her bracelet. "It—won't—come—off!"

"Give it that stupid stone!" Kara shrieked. She reached to yank it from Adriane's wrist and the wolf stone exploded with golden fire. Jagged lightning pierced the ground in front of them. The girls stared at the smoking fissure.

The monster stepped back, red eyes flashing dangerously. Then it leaped at the girls.

Something flashed past them and slammed into the creature with a sickening *thud*!

"Storm!" Adriane cried.

The monster staggered as the great wolf snarled and lunged for its throat. Grabbing the wolf, the beast twisted her head back, trying to rip it from her neck. The ball of stars floated in the air and bounced lightly away.

Adriane lunged forward.

"Adriane, no!" Emily grabbed Adriane and pulled her back.

Stormbringer's teeth raked through the monster's arm as she leaped free to rip at its leg, trying to unbalance it. The manticore whirled and knocked the wolf to the ground, pinning her under a massive foot. With a roar, it smashed a razor-clawed fist into her. Stormbringer's howl echoed into the night as she burst apart in a haze of mist and vanished.

"Storm!" Adriane screamed and tried to pull out of Emily's grasp.

"No!" Emily cried.

She and Adriane struggled and the two bracelets crashed

together. Fire erupted from the stones and blinding wild magic flew out in all directions at once. A bolt blasted into a tree, splitting it in two. The monster bellowed with fury.

Kara clutched at Adriane and Emily as magic fire streamed from the jewels, arcing into the night sky.

"Try and hold it!" Adriane called out.

"I can't!" Emily screamed.

"Stay together! All of us!" Adriane ordered.

Kara hung on to Adriane and Emily as sparks of power raced over her to fuel the magic fire. Adriane and Emily swung the stream of fire like a bat. It came around hard, smacking the manticore, knocking it across the field.

The creature curled in upon itself and fell to the ground.

Wild lightning zigzagged erratically all around them.

"I can't control it!" Emily yelled.

The air wrenched. The ground twisted. The sky cracked …

And the portal opened.

It was an immense empty space hanging in the air just off the ground. Trying to see through it was like trying to see through a thick fog. They could just make out a web of glowing lines, stars winking in complex patterns.

"You did it!" Ozzie shouted.

"Wow!" Kara looked into the endless void of the magic web.

"Hurry, get Phel up!" Ozzie was pushing at Phel's side.

The girls rushed over and gently helped Phel to his feet. He was so light they had a hard time grabbing onto him.

"Hold on, Phel! Please!" Emily called. "You're almost home!"

The web of stars twisted into a sparkling tunnel. They

pushed Phel toward it. He floated into the portal and was gone.

Emily and Ozzie looked at each other. "Go, Ozzie, take care of him."

Ozzie faced the doorway that would take him home. The twisting tunnel was already getting smaller. He looked back at the girls.

"Go, Ozzie!" Emily yelled. "Before the portal closes again!"

Ozzie leaped after Phel—and vanished.

"We love you," Emily called.

A rush of hot wind whipped the girls' hair and clothes. They clutched one another in terror as the manticore returned and swooped in to land beside the portal. Phel's twinkling ball of stars was cradled in its huge, clawed hands.

The girls backed away.

The creature held up the sparkling ball. "I will be rewarded for this prize. Though I did enjoy the hunt, and the animals were amusing sport." It grinned wickedly then turned red-hot eyes on Emily. Emily shrank back from the intense gaze and her gem flickered with dark purple.

"You have deceived yourself." The red eyes were hypnotic, and Emily felt herself falling back into those familiar feelings of despair. "Magic cannot change what you really are. You are weak and helpless and doomed to failure."

"No!" Emily cried out. She held up her gemstone. "I am a healer!"

Adriane raised her stone in the air. Kara stood between them, outstretched hands touching each of the jewels. Diamond-white blazed through her body to join the growing glow of blue-green and sun-gold.

"And no one messes with our friends!" Emily shouted as the magic built into an inferno of unearthly fire.

Fear flashed in the monster's eyes.

Blinding light streamed out of the gemstones and hammered into the manticore. Still clutching the fairy map, it fell backward into the portal. The mist closed over it.

The twisting tunnel vanished as the web of stars glowed brighter and began to expand, spreading like an immense spiderweb over the entire field. The more it spread, the thinner it became … until nothing was left but a bright star hanging in the air where the portal had been. It twinkled— and winked out.

The clearing was still and quiet. Stormbringer came padding across the grass. Adriane ran to her, hugging the wolf and burying her face in the thick fur.

Exhausted, Emily sank to the ground, covering her face.

"Ozzie did it. He got home. That's all he ever wanted," she said quietly.

"He was one brave ferret," Adriane said.

"And kinda cute, too," Kara added.

"I'm going to miss him so much," Emily cried.

"Gee, you'd think I was already dead."

The girls whirled around. The ferret was standing right behind them.

"Ozzie!" Emily got up and ran to the ferret, picking him off the ground in a sweeping hug. "What happened?" she asked. "We thought you went home."

"And miss all this excitement? With all the trouble you get into, who do you think is going to look after you three?"

"But I thought you wanted to go home," Emily said.

"I did, and here I am." Ozzie smiled.

"We lost the fairy map," Adriane said.

Ozzie shrugged. "Together we'll find another way."

"But what if the monster comes back?" Kara asked.

"It got what it wanted. But the Fairimentals also got something *they* wanted."

All three girls looked at him. "What?"

"You."

"WELCOME TO THE Ravenswood Wildlife Preserve," Gran said politely. The group gathered on the great lawn behind the manor had been oohing and ahhing over the expansive gardens, with their beautiful fountains and sculptures. Everyone turned expectantly to Gran. The entire town council was there.

"Mrs. Charday, on behalf of the town council, I'd like to thank you for inviting us to this remarkable place," Mayor Davies said formally. Beasley Windor scowled, looking around as if she expected a wild animal to jump out of a bush. "And, of course, our appreciation goes to Dr. Allison from the Centers for Disease Control in Atlanta."

Standing next to Emily's mom, the CDC health official waved. He was a tall, handsome man. Emily and Adriane stood next to Gran. Kara was not there. Since the bizarre events two weeks earlier, they hadn't seen her or heard a peep out of her.

"The Ravenswood Preserve has been a safe haven for animals for over a hundred years," Gran said. "My granddaughter, Adriane, and her friend, Emily, will take you on the tour. Hiking is a bit difficult for me," she added with a small smile.

"That's our cue," Adriane whispered as they stepped forward. "Hi, everyone. If you'll all follow me, we'll begin the tour out back here on the great lawn."

The group followed the girls across the lawn to the maze garden.

On the other side of some hedges, a family of deer watched them.

"Ooh, deer," one of the women said.

"Can we pet them?" another asked.

"Yes, they're very tame." Adriane handed around some small bags of animal feed.

The group looked to Dr. Allison.

"It's quite all right," the CDC official assured them. "These deer are perfectly healthy and quite native to these woods."

The crowd gathered round to pet and feed the deer.

Mrs. Windor stood to the side, remarking loudly about how easily these lawns could be transformed into the back nine holes of a golf course. Fellow councilman Sid Stewart nodded enthusiastically.

Ronif popped his head out of a hedge behind Emily. "How's it going?" the quiffle asked.

Emily pushed the quiffle's head back down in the bush. "What are you doing? You're supposed to be waiting with the others!"

"Everyone wants to know what's happening," said the bush.

"Fine! Now get back and make sure the others stay put," Emily whispered.

The quiffle skirted away through the bush. One of the

branches poked Beasley Windor's behind. Startled, she scowled.

Emily giggled as the group followed Adriane into a sculpture-filled water garden where peacocks strolled between the fountains, displaying their resplendent feathers. Everyone oohed and ahhhed, and Emily began to think they could really win them over.

"Oh, look!" someone cried. Heads turned skyward.

An incredible owl was perched atop a tall fountain. Emily winked, and Ariel winked back. Spreading her magnificent wings, the owl took off. She glided in slow, perfect circles over the heads of the amazed group and came to land on Emily's arm.

"How'd I doo"?

"Just wonderful!" Emily kissed the owl's head and smiled at the astonished onlookers.

"Well, Miss Fletcher, you certainly have a way with these animals," the mayor said.

Emily beamed. "Her name is Ariel. She's a snow owl, very rare." Ariel looked at the humans with huge, sparkling eyes.

The group looked to the CDC official. He laughed and gave a thumbs-up. Everyone crowded around Emily for a chance to pet the owl.

On the way back to the manor house the group buzzed with excitement. Beasley Windor was loudly suggesting the perfect place for the clubhouse when she stopped in midsentence.

In the middle of the lawn, a large silver wolf sat staring at her with golden eyes.

Beasley Windor pointed. "Aha! See? A dangerous animal!"

Adriane walked over and patted the wolf. "Please don't be frightened," she told the crowd. "I'd like you all to meet Stormbringer. She lives with us here at the preserve. We take care of her, but she really takes care of us." She smiled.

"Incredible!" someone said.

"I never knew such creatures lived out here," another commented.

"She's very friendly and loves childern." Adriane ruffled the wolf's fur.

All heads turned to Dr. Allison. He walked up and patted the great wolf. "Certainly seems healthy," he declared. "And obviously very well people-trained."

Storm stood admirably still, allowing everyone to pet and admire her.

Adriane hugged her. "You're the best!" she whispered.

"I'd rather be running with you through the forests."

"Fantastic!" Mayor Davies exclaimed, taking in a deep breath of the crisp late summer air. "I'd forgotten how invigorating being out here felt!"

"That's all well and good," Mrs. Beasley stated, "but what about the woods? How do we know it's truly safe out there?"

"There have been no attacks in the last two weeks," the mayor responded. "No reports of anything unusual, and Dr. Allison has personally checked these animals."

Carolyn stepped forward. "I've seen no sign of anything that would be cause for shutting down this preserve."

Dr. Allison spoke up. "Frankly, I haven't seen a trace of disease or toxins. Of course, something like that could still be lurking—"

"You see?" Mrs. Beasley interrupted triumphantly.

"Excuse me," the CDC man continued firmly. "Dr. Fletcher and I both agree that it could have been a diseased animal responsible for the attacks, but I've found no evidence of anything here that might pose a danger to public health. My recommendation would be to watch and wait. If anything further is detected, Dr. Fletcher will contact me, but for now I'd say you have a one-of-a-kind treasure that the whole town should be proud of. As far as the CDC is concerned, Ravenswood Wildlife Preserve gets a clean bill of health!"

"Yes!" Emily burst out as she and Adriane high-fived.

"Thank you, Dr. Allison." Beasley Windor stepped forward. "We're all very relieved at your report. However, the issue still remains. These animals can live anywhere. What the town needs is income, not animals. We need to put this to a vote, and *I* vote for the redevelopment of this land into the Stonehill Golf Course and Country Club!"

"She has a point," Sid Stewart said.

Emily's heart sank. "Oh, no!"

Adriane kicked a stone. "I knew it! Nothing ever works out!"

"Aww, you girls break a nail?"

They turned around to find Kara standing there.

"Kara!" Emily said.

"Oh, of course, you had to come and cast your vote for the country club," Adriane said snidely.

"Well, if we get one, I know I won't be seeing *you* there!" Kara shot back

Adriane fumed. Kara fumed right back at her.

"Mrs. Windor," Mayor Davies said. "Before we vote, I have a proposition for Mrs. Charday."

Everyone looked at the mayor. He pointed to Kara. "My

daughter, Kara, has suggested we open the preserve for tours, to give people a chance to see this beautiful place and learn about the animals—just like it was years ago."

"Not a bad idea," someone said.

Emily and Adriane looked at Kara.

"I told you I could talk Daddy into anything," Kara said nonchalantly.

"What do you say, Mrs. Charday?" the mayor asked.

Gran, standing with crossed arms, shook her head. She started to say no but stopped herself when she looked at Emily, Adriane, and Kara. Her expression relaxed and her eyes twinkled. "On one condition."

"Name it," the mayor asked warily.

"We'll allow the estate to be opened to the public in exchange for the town's support and protection of the preserve and its inhabitants."

"Agreed," the mayor said.

"And," Gran continued, "you will allow us to apply for official federal landmark and wildlife sanctuary status."

"That's two conditions, but I think that will fly." The mayor smiled.

"Wow," Emily said.

Mayor Davies stepped forward. "All in favor of trying out the preserve as our new town project, say 'aye.'"

A resounding chorus of ayes came from the crowd.

"All those not in favor, say 'nay.'"

Everyone looked to Beasley Windor. Her mouth flapped opened and closed, but she kept silent.

"Done!" The mayor turned to Gran, a smile on his face and his hand extended. "I think we have a deal."

Gran shook his hand.

Emily's heart did a flip. "Adriane! Landmark status! That means no one can ever shut this place down again." She turned to Kara. "Kara, I can't believe it! You are amazing!"

"Yeah … that's great, Kara." Adriane looked down at her boots.

"Yes, it is. Excuse me." Kara went to join her father.

"Congratulations." Mrs. Windor had moved in front of Emily and Adriane.

"Thank you," Emily said.

Mrs. Windor bent in close. "Your little show-and-tell didn't fool me, missy! Something is going on out here and I'm going to find out what!" She turned and stormed away.

Mayor Davies had his arm around Kara's shoulders. "I'd like to officially appoint Kara as the mayor's liaison to the new Ravenswood Preservation Society!"

Emily and Adriane looked at each other. The *what?*

The council members applauded and Kara beamed.

"Thank you," Kara said, flashing her dazzling smile over the crowd. "I have lots of ideas, starting with our first fund-raising party."

"Marvelous!" exclaimed a councilwoman. The crowd buzzed around Kara.

Emily's mind was racing. "We could set up a Web site," she spoke up, "so people all over could learn about the preserve—and about wildlife conservation."

"A Web site! Excellent!" The mayor's smile was growing wider.

"We'd certainly link to it from the Chamber of Commerce website," a council member added. "It would be a real tourist attraction!"

Adriane dragged Emily away from the crowd. "Are you

crazy! What are you talking about: Web sites! How're we going to do that? How are we going to learn about … all this?" She held up her stone.

"What do you think of our nifty club?" Kara bounded over. "Of course, I'll be president."

"Club?! This isn't the Girl Scouts!" Adriane burst out.

"Adriane, think," Emily said. "It's the perfect setup to learn about the magic."

Adriane was still mad. "You don't even have a stone," she reminded Kara.

Kara stared at the girls' jewels. "Oh, yeah, and another thing … "

"What now?" Adriane asked.

"I need my own jewel."

"It's a good start," the mayor was saying to the others. He waved his arm over to Emily, Adriane, and Kara. "And we've got a great team here to supervise."

"And it has to be big and sparkly like a diamond." Kara smiled a dazzling smile at Adriane.

"Why don't I just get out the magic carpet and we'll fly around and find one?" Adriane suggested sarcastically.

"You got one? I need that, too."

Emily had to laugh. Kara and Adriane were from such different worlds. If they could ever work things out, they might actually make a great team.

She looked across at the woods. She thought about how far she had come from that girl left behind 2,500 miles across the country, and what she had lost along the way. But Emily realized she had also found something. She was a healer and healers found hope.

There was so much to learn, a future so full of

possibilities. Maybe Kara could find a magic stone of her own. Maybe Ozzie could find a way back into his real body. She looked at Adriane, so full of fire. A "warrior." Maybe she would find her true path.

The mystery of the web and the fairy map danced across her mind. What roads would it take her down? She thought of Phel and hoped he was safe. Maybe it was possible there existed a place where dreams came true. A place of magic where all creatures were safe. Was *that* what Avalon was?

She looked at her jewel. A soft aqua glow pulsed briefly. She smiled and looked back at her friends. Emily was no longer afraid of her future. Wherever it may lead, she knew she wouldn't be going there alone.

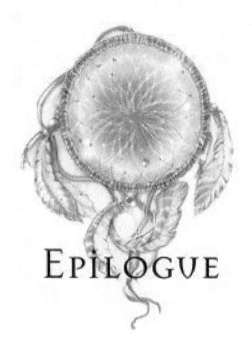

EPILOGUE

THE CAT WATCHED from the trees. Emily's magic had helped her more than the girl knew. Of course, Emily had a sense of the magic only, not real knowledge yet. But that was okay, because the cat didn't belong with her. She belonged with the other one.

The cat purred and licked her paw. She and the other animals were in Ravenswood, away from the poison that was spreading across their own land. And they'd found the ones who would help them—the three: the healer, the warrior, and the blazing star. There was hope for her world after all.

Still, they were not safe. The manticore would likely be back and more like it would come—creatures just as evil, just as dangerous ... or worse. The Dark Sorceress would never stop. She would drain all the magic from Aldenmor, Earth, and all the worlds throughout the magic web … all the way to Avalon itself.

The cat was suddenly tired. Her eyes felt heavy. They closed with the knowledge that it was all just beginning.

Bestiary & Creature Guide

STORMBRINGER
AFFILIATION: GOOD

Storm is a mistwolf that has bonded with Adriane. Mistwolves are shape-shifters, able to change to shadowy fog and clouds, becoming practically invisible.

Storm's bloodline goes back thousands years, enabling her to tap into memories and visions of the past. Noble, courageous, and true of heart, Storm is a true warrior, always ready to protect her friends.

JEERAN
AFFILIATION: NEUTRAL

Jeeran are beautiful deer-like animals with long ears, purple eyes, and soft green-striped fur. Agile and fast, Jeeran are originally from the hills and forests of the Moorgroves, but have found their way into many of the forested regions across all of Aldenmor. They are thought to be sentient but keep to themselves.

PEGASUS

AFFILIATION: GOOD

Pegasi are magnificent winged steeds, intelligent creatures, shy and wild and not easily tamed. When they do bond, they serve their friends with absolute faithfulness.

QUIFFLE
AFFILIATION: GOOD

Silver duck-like creatures that flourish throughout the lakes and wetlands of Aldenmor. Quiffles are intelligent and fun-loving with strong family bonds. They are also loyal friends and allies to the other good animals of Aldenmor.

ABOUT THE AUTHOR

Rachel Roberts loves magic, music, adventure, and animals. She lives in sunny southern California with two cats, Attila and Raider.

Rachel's been reading since she could first hold a book and loves getting lost in a great story. She has been a writer and editor her entire professional life. Rachel also loves music, and plays the piano, flute, and is learning to play guitar.

Avalon: Web of Magic is Rachel's first series of novels.

The Adventure Continues With Book 2
All That Glitters

THE UNICORN STOOD in the woodland meadow. His deep golden eyes were wary but unafraid. Wildflowers blanketed the field in bright colors as Kara walked toward the magnificent creature. The unicorn raised his glimmering crystal horn, filling the meadow with flashes of brilliant light.

Kara circled the great creature. He was breathtakingly beautiful. She ran a hand over his lustrous white hide; it felt soft as silk and shimmered gently. Breathing slowly, the unicorn lowered his head as Kara came around to look into his eyes.

His voice suddenly filled her head.

"I am for the blazing star."

She was special. If anyone were to ride a unicorn, of course it would be her.

With a leap, she was on his back.

The unicorn took off, racing across the open field. Confident, Kara leaned forward into the creature's steady gallop, feeling herself one with the animal, just as she had been taught at riding school. But this was no ordinary animal. This was the most magical of all creatures. The unicorn raced through the meadow and leaped. Instantly a portal opened—a circle of swirling stars hanging in the air before them—and the unicorn swept through.

Kara was bathed in diamond light as endless loops woven together in intricate patterns revealed itself before her: the magic web that connected worlds. Together Kara and the unicorn ran, faster ... faster ... streaking across the infinite web of magic.

"Come to me ... " Another voice, distant yet commanding, cut through her mind like steel.

The unicorn raced along the web like white fire.

She was a golden girl, adored by all. She was a goddess, born to be with such a magnificent creature.

"You will be mine ... "

She was a princess of magic ... No! She was a ... queen!

" ... or everything you love will die!"

The unicorn stumbled. Kara flew headlong, golden hair tangling as she tossed and turned. A dark-robed figure watched, indifferent, as Kara fell, a shooting star fading into darkness.

Kara's eyes sprang open. It was pitch-black. Her heart pounded. For a second she couldn't move, then realized she was completely tangled in her bed sheets. She wriggled and kicked them off, ripping her pink satin sleep mask from her eyes.

At first she thought that the cold had awakened her, since the hairs along her arms and the back of her neck were standing up. But the room was humid, too warm for comfort. Blearily, she pushed her hair out of her face and looked around.

Pale moonlight glazed the room, glowing softly through the curtains as they wavered in the breeze. The air-conditioning must have gone out, she thought, burrowing back into her pillow. But then there wouldn't be a breeze, would there? As her brain fought its way to sense, she sat up.

The far window was wide open.

Puzzled, Kara stumbled over to shut the window. Had she forgotten before? She'd been pretty tired ... She stopped short. The window screen was gone. She peered into the darkness, but nothing moved, no sound broke the stillness. The screen must have fallen off somehow, she thought. Then she saw something on the ledge below her window: splotches of glowing, green muck, dripping into the gutter.

That's disgusting! How dare some big bird drop a surprise on their roof!

She closed the window with a bang and locked it. Shaken, she climbed back into bed, adjusted her sleep mask, and went back to sleep.

In the dark beyond the window, two piercing green eyes stared back at her, then winked out.

AvALon
WEB OF MAGIC

AVAILABLE NOW

COMING SOON

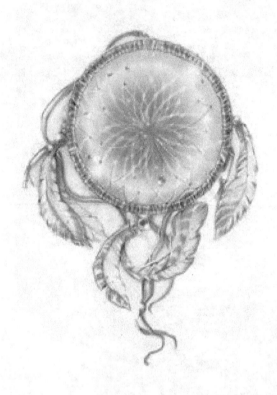